He reached out and gently cupped her face, drawing her close

Then he slowly captured her mouth. She moaned instantly as the tender kiss deepened. She melted against his body and her heartbeat quickened.

The man kissed like he'd invented the technique. His tongue pressed against her lips. He immediately delved deeper into her mouth as her body relaxed against his. She moaned, feeling a tremor course through her. Her heart raced and her skin tingled. The taste of him was like nectar and she imbibed his flavor in a ravenous surrender. He fed her passion and she greedily indulged. He was doing things to her—things she'd forgotten were even possible.

CELESTE O. NORFLEET

a native Philadelphian, has always been artistic, but now her artistic imagination flows through the computer keys instead of a paintbrush. She is a prolific writer for Kimani Arabesque and Kimani Romance. Her romance novels, realistic with a touch of humor, depict strong sexy characters with unpredictable plots and exciting story lines. With an impressive backlist, she continues to win rave reviews and critical praise for her spicy sexy romances that scintillate, as well as entertain. Celeste also lends her talent to the Kimani TRU young adult line. Her young adult novels are dramatic fiction, reflecting current issues facing all teens. Celeste has been nominated for numerous awards. She lives in Virginia with her husband and two teens. You can visit Celeste's website, www.celesteonorfleet.com, contact her at conorfleet@aol.com or P.O. Box 7346, Woodbridge, VA 22195-7346.

Just One
Touch

CELESTE O.
NORFLEET

KIMANI
ROMANCE

To Fate & Fortune

KIMANI PRESS™

ISBN-13: 978-0-373-86221-4

Recycling programs
for this product may
not exist in your area.

JUST ONE TOUCH

www.kimanipress.com

Printed in U.S.A.

Dear Reader,

In writing *Just One Touch*, I got to research and experience the beauty and awesome splendor of Martha's Vineyard. It was a dream come true, since I also got to continue the Coles family series with Tatiana Coles on the island for the summer. Tia, as she is affectionately called, finds rekindled love with Spencer Cage to be more than she expected and even more than she hoped. I love the idea of joining two hearts to renew a lost love. For these two lovers, *Just One Touch* is all it takes to send the mercury rising. So fair warning—this book is hot and sexy. So grab something cold, relax in your favorite place and as always…enjoy!

Watch for *Lover's Paradise* coming in December 2011. Mamma Lou is back on Crescent Island and she's ready for more matchmaking before she walks down the aisle.

Blessings & Peace,

Celeste O. Norfleet

Chapter 1

Tatiana Coles turned the doorknob and was surprised to find the front door unlocked. She figured it was okay, so she walked in. After all, the guesthouse cottage was all hers and her sisters' for the next thirty days. She'd gotten the key from the owners—the Sullivans—who were friends of her parents. Her timing was perfect. They were leaving for their month-long cruise just as she was arriving. The Sullivans had been running late and apologized for being so abrupt, but that was just fine with Tatiana. The last thing she needed was questions about her job, and she knew Mr. Sullivan—a retired news reporter—was bound to be a little suspicious. Her boss was still trying to contact her. And she knew there'd be ramifications when she got back, but right now she didn't care. All she cared about was thirty days of drama-free relaxation, sun, sand and beach.

Still, every time she thought about the assignment they had wanted her to take in Paris she fumed. She was a journalist, not a babysitter. For the first two and a half years of her career, she'd traveled the world reporting on important issues. She'd interviewed heads of state, business and industry leaders, national politicians and celebrities, covering everything from the economy to the war to healthcare. Her byline and reputation were among the most highly regarded in the media.

Then six months ago everything changed. One stupid corporate executive propositioned her after an interview, and she'd turned him down. As a result, he filed a libel suit against the media company she worked for, mostly because her article had made him look foolish— although that's not what the lawsuit alleged. Either way, she was relegated to writing puff pieces and filler until the whole thing blew over or the CEO dropped his suit.

The reason her boss gave her for being demoted was even more insulting. He'd said she wasn't up to the challenge of interviewing anymore. But the last straw had been the Paris assignment: she was being sent to watch over one of the news magazine's worst reporters. He was slated to interview the alleged head of a terrorist group tied to a recent string of violent attacks.

It was insane. She knew he had no idea how to conduct the interview or what to ask. Still he'd gotten the assignment. In protest, she'd decided to abruptly take a leave of absence. It was hasty, childish, impulsive and unprofessional, but she didn't care. Lately, she didn't care much about a lot of things in her life. She was aggravated and stressed and in need of some serious down time. And the temporary leave was perfect.

"Hey! Surprise! Guess who's here," she called out, holding the door open with her hip as she noisily stumbled inside. Loaded down with two large suitcases, she rolled them in front of the door to keep it propped open and then placed her laptop and handbag on the floor beside her luggage.

"Nikita? Natalia? Anybody! How about a little help?" she yelled louder this time, somehow managing to maneuver the suitcases inside the door and close it behind her. She paused, catching her breath, and took a quick look around. The Sullivans—Jeff and Theresa—were her parents' friends. They owned the summer house and the small cottage next to it on a private beach in Martha's Vineyard. For years, the Coles would visit them in the Vineyard during the summertime, and the Sullivans would visit the Coles in Key West in the winter. After college, Tatiana's brothers used to rent the Sullivan's beach cottage for a month. But in the last five years, she and her sisters had taken over the summer rental. Now, every year for the month of August, it was all theirs.

"Niki, Nat, you guys around?" she called out as she grabbed her purse and laptop and put them on the table behind the sofa. There was no reply. "Niki, Nat," she called out again, expecting one or both of her sisters to answer. She rolled her suitcases to the bottom of the stairs. She drew in a deep breath and then exhaled slowly as a contented, easy smile spread across her lips. Thank God she was finally here. After hours of traveling, all she could think about was relaxing on the beach. Looking out at the ocean view, all the craziness she'd endured to get there was certainly worth it. Hanging out with her sisters always revived her spirit and she was definitely in need of that now.

"Nikita, Natalia." She went upstairs and peeked into each of the three bedrooms. The beds were perfectly made, as if they hadn't been slept in for days. She took the same bedroom she usually did, freshened up, changed into a purple bikini and slipped on a pair of baggy sweatpants. Afterward, she took off her ponytail clip and ran her fingers through her long curls as she walked over to the window. Pulling the sheers back, she looked out at the vast cerulean sky. Dusk was looming and the view from the window was spectacular and serene. She hadn't realize how much she missed being here. She went back downstairs, grabbed her cell and turned it on for the first time in hours to call her sister Nikita.

The call went directly to voice mail. "Hey, where are you? I hope you're out grabbing something to eat because I'm starved. I haven't eaten anything since I left London. That was nearly sixteen hours ago. I'm thinking seafood. Call me," she said, leaving a message.

She slipped her phone into the pocket of her sweat-pants and looked around, this time more attentively. It had been years since she'd been here last and it seemed that everything about the place in the Vineyard had changed. The only thing she remembered being the same was the large stone fireplace in the living room. It was made of old mason stones left in their rugged, natural state. It was the cornerstone of the room. She walked over and rubbed her hand along the rough edges.

Tatiana fondly remembered the summers spent at the cottage when she was young. She and her siblings would hide notes in a loose stone just below the mantel. It was their little secret. Looking at the fireplace, she wondered if their cubbyhole was still there. She strug-gled with the large stone, trying to pry it a loose. It usu-ally came out easily, but this time it didn't. So much for childhood memories.

She turned to look at the open floor plan of the family room. At one time the cottage had a distinctly rustic style. But a few years ago the Sullivans renovated the house so that it had a more contemporary design, much like a casually elegant resort. The furniture was comfortable with an eclectic mix of modern and organic pieces. The two small windows she'd remembered from years past were now a wall of French doors with panes of glass above the doorframe angled under the eaves of the house, which allowed more sunlight to stream into the great room. Overhead, large ceiling fans hung from the massive beams in the vaulted ceiling that was punctuated with recessed lights.

Tatiana opened the French doors to let the fresh air clear the stuffiness out of the cottage. The day was nearly over and the heat had not let up. She took a deep breath filling her lungs with the salty air of the Vineyard, and thought how good it was to be back. It was good to be anywhere, she thought, as she stepped out onto the back porch.

A sultry breeze enveloped her as the sweet smell of fresh flowers brought back so many memories. In a flash, the sky had suddenly changed. The horizon was a stunning vibrant mix of bright reds, purples and blues. From the porch, she could see a large expanse of white-sand beach that receded with the tide. Just as she stepped down from the porch, her cell phone rang. She checked the caller ID, sat down on one of the outdoor chairs, put her cell on the table and put the call on speakerphone. "Hey, girl," she said smiling.

"Hey, Tia, I was gonna call you later this evening. How are you?" her sister, Nikita asked.

It was always good to hear Nikita's voice. "I'm tired, stressed-out and jetlagged. Unfortunately I didn't sleep on the way here. I guess I'm too wired."

"Sounds about right for you. So, what's up?"

"What's up is that I'm here. Where are you?" Tia said, picking up on the distraction in her sister's voice. There were loud voices and the clatter of dishes in the background. Wherever her sister was, it was really noisy.

"What do you mean you're here? You're where?" Nikita asked, in a louder voice.

"I'm in Martha's Vineyard at the Sullivan's cottage. They left on a month-long cruise. We're supposed to be hanging out here for the next thirty days, remember."

"Yeah, of course I remember. I'm just surprised you're there. You said you weren't going to the Vineyard this year."

"I know. I changed my mind. Didn't you get my email?"

"Girl, I haven't read my emails in more than a week and a half. I barely have time to answer the phone anymore."

"It's so loud there. I can barely hear you. Where are you?" she asked picking up the cell phone and walking down the steps of the porch toward the water. She looked around admiring the view.

"I'm at work. I'm catering a party."

"At work, you mean in Key West?" she asked.

"Of course in Key West, where else?" Niki said.

"So, I guess you're gonna be a little late getting here," Tia said sarcastically as she followed the same path she had remembered taking over the years. She stopped and looked down at the private beach that lay ahead.

Nikita hesitated a moment. "Actually, I'm not coming."

"What do you mean, you're not coming?" Tia asked,

her stomach twisting into a knot. She had been looking forward to this break. Without realizing it, she
started walking toward the beach. It wasn't until she
was midway between the cottage and the shoreline that
she realized what she was doing. She kept going.

"Tia, it's crazy here. I have so much work to do. I
can't up and leave right now, just like that."

"Hold up, I came all the way here from London to
hang out with my sisters. I understand why Nat's not
coming. She just married the perfect man. But you, too?
I can't believe this. You're gonna just up and leave me
stranded?"

"Oh, no, you don't," Niki quickly responded. "Don't
even try it. Don't you dare put this off on me or Nat.
You're the one who said you couldn't get away this year
just like last year and the year before that and the year
before that. You're the one who's always too busy working, remember? Nat and I were in the Vineyard three
summers straight without you."

Tia knew her sister was right. She was the one who'd
always begged off. She'd done it before, but her unexpected problems at work made her change her plans.
"Okay, okay, I know. But I'm here now. So, can you
come?" She looked around at the secluded area. She
kicked off her sandals, picked them up from the sand
and started walking toward the water.

"I can't," Niki said woefully, "At least not for a few
days, maybe a week or so. Since Nat's wedding, the catering requests have been nonstop. I'm so busy I've had

to put everything else in my life on hold, including my expansion plans. I had to hire two new people in the café and get an assistant to help with scheduling."

"Niki, that's fantastic. I'm really happy for you, but you know you can't work all the time. Everybody needs to take a break every now and then. All work and no play…"

Nikita started laughing. Tia didn't have to ask why. She knew she sounded like a hypocrite. Aside from their two brothers, Mikhail and Dominik, Tia was even more of a workaholic than her two sisters. "Okay, okay, it wasn't that funny," Tia said, looking around as Niki continued laughing. A seagull flying overhead caught her attention. She looked up, watching its flight path. It swooped down low across the water then soared higher into the sky across the beach. "I guess I'll just have to do some sightseeing or find a distraction until you get here." As soon as the words left her mouth her gaze shifted as something—or rather *someone*—near the water's edge caught her attention. "Hello, distraction," she muttered admiringly.

"What, wait, hold on, Tia, I need to get something out of the oven."

"Yeah, go ahead," she said, suddenly fascinated by the man standing near the shoreline. How could she have missed him before? He was just a short distance away talking on a cell phone walking just beyond the incoming tide. His back was to her, but even so she could see there was something about him. She nibbled her lower lip as she sized him up, a quality she excelled at as a reporter.

What a person wore, how they stood or walked, spoke volumes, even before they said a word. He wore loose-fitting white pants and a white shirt with the sleeves rolled up midway on his arms. His shirt flapped in the warm breeze. He was barefoot and he looked to be quite muscular with broad shoulders, a narrow waist and slightly bowed legs.

She watched with interest each movement he made. He walked a few steps then stopped and stood with his legs apart in an arrogant and confident way. He exuded power. She arched her brow with added interest as she nodded approvingly. Although something about him seemed oddly familiar, she dismissed the thought. She certainly would have remembered seeing him before.

Unable to see his face, it was his body that drew her in. There was something overtly masculine and sexy about him. He appeared tall, dark and built for just the fantasy she had in mind—sex on the beach. She smiled. *Um-um good.* Perhaps a Vineyard romance wasn't such a bad idea after all. It just might be the distraction she needed until her sister arrived.

Since it was a private beach, she knew he was more than likely a neighbor or guest of someone in the private enclave. That meant it was her neighborly duty to go over and introduce herself. She started walking toward him.

"I'm back. Okay, sightseeing, *distraction?*" Nikita

repeated skeptically as soon as she picked up the phone again. "Come on, Tia, we've been going to Martha's Vineyard almost all our lives. I think you've seen just about everything worth seeing and then some. What's left?"

Tia chuckled to herself while appreciating her new-found interest. He was undeniably milk-chocolate decadence wrapped in the perfect package. "That's not the kind of distraction I was talking about."

Niki started laughing. "Well it's about time you got your freak on. How long has it been, five months, seven?"

"Fifteen months, but who's counting?"

"Fifteen months without sex! Good Lord, Tia, no wonder you're all stressed out. I get the whole adventurous spirit and all. But girl, you need to get your pipes flushed for real."

Tia laughed. "Pipes flushed? Really, Niki, is that the best you can come up with?" Niki laughed, too. "Now come on, you have to admit it's not so strange for a woman to abstain from sex for a while. You know women go without sex all the time, even you."

"True, but fifteen months is a long, lonely time. And besides, I have an excuse. I'm extremely picky. Word to the wise—men excel at two things, sex and breaking hearts. Enjoy the first and avoid the latter. Just make sure you don't put your heart out there. Remember my mantra: love 'em and leave 'em."

Tia shook her head ruefully. Her sister's *love 'em and*

leave 'em philosophy had been her relationship M.O. for far too long. Niki was definitely the queen of "stay away from love." Two years ago, her fiancé left her at the altar. There was no letter, no phone call, no nothing. She was broken-hearted and devastated. Her pain turned into anger and then festered. She'd been licking her wounds ever since. Men had tried to get close, but she kept them at arm's-length. Tia often wondered if there was any man out there who could mend her sister's broken heart.

"Are you man-bashing again?"

"No way. I love men. You know that. I just love them lying on their backs even better."

Tia laughed. She knew her sister didn't really mean it. It was just her heartache talking.

"Never mind about me, you go flush your pipes. I'll be there in a week or so. You can tell me all about it when I get there."

The man on the cell phone turned toward her so that she could make out his profile. Another spark of recognition swept over her. She stopped walking. It couldn't be. He'd never come to Martha's Vineyard. She quickly dismissed the idea and continued walking toward him. She was probably feeling the effects of jetlag or, like her sister said, her fifteen-month sexual hiatus was finally getting to her.

"Sounds good to me," she answered, "and I think I just found the perfect—" She stopped cold. He turned toward her a little more. Her stomach dropped as if she'd taken a free fall from atop a mile-high roller coaster ride. She removed her dark sunglasses and squinted. No, it wasn't him, she tried convincing herself. It couldn't be. He was less muscular and much taller, besides she knew for a fact that he was doing a video on the West Coast. It wasn't that she'd followed his every move so much as she'd made sure their paths never crossed again. Part of that involved her knowing exactly where he was at all times. She slowly relaxed. A moment later she stopped after hearing his voice. *"Reject the offer. My company's not for sale."* Then she froze midstep seeing the tattoo, their tattoo.

Oh, my God. It is him.

Niki laughed, but Tia had stopped listening. She'd stopped everything. In an instant her past had caught up to her. She stood perfectly still as if even the slightest movement would prompt him to turn in her direction. He started walking away. She took a deep breath and held it. There was no other man who walked like that, stood like that and made her body feel like it did. An overwhelming feeling of trepidation and tension coursed through her body. She was completely unnerved. Her stomach clenched and then quivered. It was him. She took a step back. There was no way she was ready for this. Not now. Not ever.

He hadn't seen her yet, so if she turned around now she could probably walk back to the porch unnoticed. The coward in her wanted to run, but she knew she couldn't. In the last three years she had reported from war zones and faced terrorist attacks. She had confronted them all with fearlessness. No panic. But there was no way she could face this.

"Niki, let me call you back," she said softly. "There's somebody here who I don't want to…" The words faded as he turned. He quickly glanced in her direction as he continued walking. Then he stopped, turned and looked right at her. He saw her and she knew it. Her heart shuddered and her stomach clenched again. Heaven help her, he hadn't changed a bit. He was still the most gorgeous sight on the planet. Everything she remembered and everything she loved was standing just a few feet away staring right back at her.

"Don't want to what?" Niki said. "Tia?"

"Niki, I'll talk to you later." She took a deep breath and just stood there. She didn't move. She didn't blink. She didn't even breathe. Her mouth went dry and every nerve in her body tensed. It had been three long years since she'd seen him. In that time their paths had never crossed. She'd made sure of that. She knew how to stay away, and living on another continent definitely made it easier. But now, face-to-face, she couldn't resist seeing him just one more time.

He'd stopped walking and just stood there staring. She took a step back, but retreat wasn't in her arsenal. There was no way she'd just walk away as if she hadn't seen him. He started walking toward her slowly—each foot perfectly aligned, one in front of the other. His cool confident swagger was unmistakable. Her body heated as each step closed the gap between them. Within seconds they stood face-to-face.

Chapter 2

Tia bit her lower lip and gazed admiringly at the man approaching her. Her eyes slowly swept over his face, down his body then back to his face. He looked different, but still very much the same. His chiseled features were hard and angular, yet classically good-looking. Now, as she looked closer, he seemed more mature. His dark hair was still cut short, but now his perfect jaw line was framed with more than a five o'clock shadow. It looked good on him.

His mouth, with its tempting full lips, was still perfectly bowed. Her stomach fluttered just thinking about the things he did to her with his mouth. And those eyes—good Lord, have mercy—his dark, sexy bedroom eyes should have been outlawed. They were black as sin and framed by long, thick lashes that would make a supermodel jealous. When he gazed into her eyes, heaven help her, he could penetrate any defense she had. He had a way of knowing what she was feeling, even if she didn't know herself.

She looked down at his well-developed chest, his muscled arms, his flat stomach, his narrow waist and the tiny hairs that disappeared at his waistband. The man was pure masculinity. She remembered the last time she'd seen him. His naked body was sprawled across a bed. The thought hit her hard. She could feel her body reacting to him. Hormones surged and juices flowed. A sudden blazing quiver rippled through her body as a wave of goose-bumps pricked her skin.

She looked up and gazed into his eyes. How could she not? They were hypnotic. He was pure seduction. Every fantasy she'd ever had started right there in his bedroom eyes. He hadn't just been her lover. He was the man she was in love with. The man who had taught her everything she ever knew about love, passion and desire. He was also the man who taught her about betrayal, abandonment and deceit.

"Spencer Cage," she said barely above a whisper. Her voice was low, and laced with apprehension.

"Tatiana Coles," he responded. Neither spoke for a few seconds. "It's been a long time," he said. His face was stern and hard as if set in stone, and yet the deep dimple in his left cheek teased as he spoke.

"Yes, it has. Three years," she confirmed.

"How's the family?" he asked. His cell phone vibrated.

"Good, great. Everybody's fine, working hard. My brothers are doing well. Niki's café is set to expand and Natalia just got married."

"Yes, I know, to Greg Montgomery. He's a good friend. Unfortunately, I couldn't attend. He's a very lucky man. I know from experience the Coles women are well worth a man's heart."

She didn't reply. "So where are *the guys?*" she asked, looking around the beach.

"What *guys?*" he asked, as his cell phone vibrated again.

"The crew. You know, your entourage—Riley, Donavan and Drill?" Tia continued. Spencer had always been surrounded by his college buddy and the close-knit group of 'round-the-way friends he had grown up with. They started out together, but Spencer's career took off. He stopped putting out music and started producing and created what became SCE.

Spencer was CEO and president of Spencer Cage Enterprises—or SCE, as it was known in the industry. SCE was a holding company with recording, production, management and promotions subsidiaries. Its stable included television, film, recording and songwriting talent. In essence, his company did it all and Spencer was poised to become the next media mogul.

He shrugged. "I'm sure they're around someplace."

"That's different. The four of you were inseparable."

He smiled and chuckled. "That was a while ago. Things change. Riley is doing his thing as an artist. He's set to begin touring this fall. Donavan's still doing his hip-hop thing. Drill is producing and managing, holding everything together. But as far as the *crew* is concerned, I'm not into the group thing anymore. Like you said before, it's just too much noise."

Tia nodded. It was exactly what she'd said to him years ago. Back then Spencer was always surrounded by his friends, and they had a tendency to confuse friendship with unanimity. Everything was by committee, and the loudest one usually led the pack. Unfortunately, the loudest wasn't necessarily the smartest.

"If you remember, there were five of us," he reminded her. His voice had an edge.

She nodded and stepped back. This was the conversation she knew was coming. It was unavoidable. "Yes, I know. I remember." She looked away then back at him. He was staring right at her. "I was sorry to hear about Mason," she said softly. "He was a character."

He smiled tightly and shook his head. She could see his anger spike. "A character," he repeated. "I mean, is that all you have to say about him?"

"Spencer, I know you're angry and upset about everything that happened. I'm sorry you feel that way. But I had no idea…"

He laughed. "Angry and upset, that's definitely an understatement. You wrote a book that ripped a man's life apart. It destroyed him and everything he had and all you can say now is that you're sorry and he was a *character?*"

There was a long silence between them. "Why did he leave you his shares of the company, *my company?*"

"I don't know."

"I think you do. Mason never did anything without a damn good reason. He left all his stock to you. One third of my company is yours. Why?"

"His reason went with him to his grave and neither one of us can change that," Tia said, solemnly.

There was another drawn-out silence. "You once told me your career was more important than anything else in your life," said Spencer. "I hope you're happy, and you got exactly what you wanted." His cell vibrated again.

"To be honest, I didn't," she said, "not even close. I had to make a choice between my feelings and my professional obligations. I did what I had to do. I hope you never have to make that choice." She looked down at the phone still in his hand. "Maybe you'd better get that. I have to go, anyway. Goodbye, Spencer." She turned and walked away.

"Tatiana, stop, wait a minute," he said, as he walked toward her.

She stopped walking, but didn't turn around. He walked over and stood behind her and placed his hands on her arms. She shivered at the feel of his touch. Her heart skipped a beat. "Tatiana, look, I'm sorry. I didn't mean to attack you like that. Seeing you here... I'm sorry. Are you okay?" he asked. The sincerity in his voice was unmistakable.

She nodded as her stomach quivered. His deep masculine voice echoed through her body. She swallowed hard then turned her head to the side slowly without turned completely around. "Yes, I'll be fine. I always am, right?" He released her and she walked away.

The pain in her heart nearly overflowed. She knew he was still standing there watching her. *Don't turn around. Don't turn around,* she repeated to herself. When she finally reached the porch, she spared a quick glance over her shoulder. He was still standing there watching her. She turned and walked inside the cottage leaving her past behind once again.

Spencer watched her go inside. He considered heading back, but he couldn't move. The sweet sway of her hips and the bounce of the loose curls on her neck had him mesmerized and riveted in place. Touching her had ignited a sexual fire as adrenaline surged through his veins. He subconsciously licked his lips. Even in his frustration and anger, she aroused him. He still wanted her and he knew nothing would ever change that. How a woman could affect him so completely was beyond him. He was furious, yet he still craved her.

He shook his head. She hadn't changed a bit. She was headstrong, stubborn and infuriating. Unlike other women he'd dated who catered to his every whim, she challenged him at every turn. She stimulated him on every level, intellectually, spiritually and physically.

He watched as she reached the porch and turned around. He nodded. She didn't respond. He smiled thinking about the expression on her face when she first recognized him. She looked just as stunned to see him as he was to see her. He'd never seen her thrown off guard before. She was always so self-assured. He was amused by her reaction. He liked the idea of surprising her.

He thought about the last time they were together. It was a memory that would never fade. They had made love the night before. Yet she never said a word about what was about to happen. The next morning she left his bed. Later that same day the biography she'd written about Mason was released. He immediately read it and was horrified. She'd called him several times that day, but he refused to answer. The relationship ended. Shortly thereafter, she left for London and he decided to avoid ever seeing her again. After that she became the itch he couldn't scratch. No one ever replaced her in his heart, no one ever would. His cell rang again as his memories faded away. This time he answered. "Yeah?"

"Yo, I'm at the house. Where you at, man?" said Drill, his best friend, business manager, bodyguard and lately his moral compass. He smiled at the irony of it all.

Growing up, Drill was the meanest, toughest thug on the block. He'd fight anyone for any reason. But years of watching his friends getting killed over nothing stemmed his appetite for violence. Now he was a dormant volcano. Still, no one was fool enough to challenge him.

"I'm on the beach."

"Your boy Frank just called the house phone. He said you weren't picking up your cell. He needs to talk to you. He said he'd call back in fifteen minutes." He paused a few seconds then continued. "You know I think what you're doing is a waste of time."

"Yeah, I know," Spencer said, knowing Drill disagreed with his plan. Frank McDermott was Spencer's personal attorney and he was using him to find out what Tia intended to do with her shares in his company. If she was going to sell, he wanted to be the first to know about it. By some twist of fate, Tia had been left shares in SCE in Mason's will. "Do me a favor. Get the studio set up, I have a few ideas I want to work out this evening."

"A'ight, you want to listen to a new artist?"

"No," he said tersely, "set it up to record."

"Yo, man, you a'ight? You sound strange."

"I'm fine," he said regaining his calm.

"A'ight, so, are you gonna actually hit up the club tonight? The party's for you so you gonna be there, right?"

"Yeah, I know, but it'll be late. I want to get in the studio tonight. I need to do some recording."

"Recording in the studio?" Drill repeated. "With who?"

"Me."

"Whoa," Drill said surprised to hear Spencer talking about going into the studio to do his own music. "Man, you haven't been in the studio putting down tracks in over five years."

"Yeah, how about that," said Spencer. "Lately, I've been feeling like doing my music."

"You mean your own release?"

"Yeah, you think the world is ready to hear from me again?"

"Hell, yeah! A'ight now. I like that, sounds good to me."

"Anything else going on?" Spencer asked.

"Yeah, heads up tonight. Donavan's gonna be there and he's looking for you. He wants face time with you for his new project. He found another female rapper he wants to produce. He's threatening to take her directly to a major label if you pass on it this time."

Spencer groaned. Technically, Donavan was his business partner, since his rich father bought shares in SCE. But he would forever be on the fringe of Spencer's tight-knit crew. Donavan might have owned a percentage of Cage Enterprises, but Spencer didn't trust him. They'd known each other since college. But Donavan always saw their relationship as *keeping your friends close and your enemies closer.* "Fine, let him."

"You know Donavan's got the inside track since his father heads a major label. He's biding his time. He wants his own thing."

"No, he doesn't want his own thing," Spencer said.

"He wants *my* thing and always has. But Cage Enterprises is not for sale."

"You know that's right," Drill said adamantly.

Even though he said the words, Spencer knew it wasn't a sure thing. All Donavan had to do was get Tia's shares in the company, secure major-label backing and he could conceivably takeover SCE. Mason leaving his shares to Tia in his will was like a noose hanging over his head. At any minute things could change and he could lose everything he'd worked so hard to achieve.

Donavan wanted power. He wanted to play in the big leagues, but he didn't know how to run a company and never took responsibility for his actions. He wanted it all, starting with Cage Enterprises. Still, hearing it out loud from Drill made him tense. "Donavan's got poor judgment and he makes business decisions with the wrong head. That's no way to stay on top."

"The important thing is he doesn't have the shares he needs and there is no way he's gonna get 'em. I don't believe Tia would sell to him or anyone else."

"Maybe, maybe not. Frank has contacted her several times, but she refuses to talk about her plans."

"Then chill, leave it alone."

"There's still the chance she could sell."

"Fine, so maybe you need to connect with her personally."

Spencer knew what Drill was implying. But after their last meeting, he was pretty sure Tia wouldn't sell to him, either. But pretty sure wasn't a hundred-percent certain. He realized he needed to make some moves to regain control of his company once and for all. Going back in the studio was the first step, but he needed something more. "Connect personally…maybe you're right," he said, looking toward Tia's beach house.

"A'ight, that's it. What's up with you, man? First you're going back in the studio to work on your first CD in five years and now you're taking my advice about getting back with Tia, what's up?" Drill said, sensing something was wrong.

Spencer took a deep breath debating whether or not to tell his friend about his encounter with Tia. It didn't matter since he'd find out eventually. "Tia's here."

There was a brief pause then a light chuckle. "Damn, you mean *your* Tia? She's here?" Drill said. "Where? On the Vineyard?"

"Yes, just now. We bumped into each other on the beach."

"Damn, is that shit fate or what. Man, the universe is talking to you. You'd better listen this time. You're getting another chance."

"This isn't about another chance. It just means she's here, that's all."

"So, that's why you're hitting the studio tonight. That girl always got your butt writing them platinum hits. For real, you need to be paying that woman serious royalties. She has more to do with your number one hits than you do. So, where is she staying?"

Spencer turned and squinted in the direction of the cottage. "She's staying at one of the houses down the beach."

"How does she look?"

"She looks good," he said, matter-of-factly, knowing that *good* was an understatement.

"What do you mean, she looks good?" Drill asked.

"All right, she looks better than good. She looks incredible."

"Yeah, I thought so. She was beautiful before, so she could only have gotten better with time. You know what I always liked about her, besides the fact that she's gorgeous, smart and talented? She's for real, man. She never pretended, not as far as I could tell. Man, she had your number good. You were seriously whipped." Drill started chuckling.

"I wouldn't say that," Spencer responded, defensively.

"I would," Drill said still chuckling. "And the thing is she's still in your blood.

"No, you're wrong. I don't have feelings for Tia, not anymore. All that's behind me, I have other things to deal with now that she's back."

"Yeah, like hooking up," Drill said.

"No, like if she can write a book filled with lies about Mason to further her career, she's capable of anything, including selling the shares Mason left her to someone like Donavan." His voice was cold. His meaning was clear.

"Oh, shit," Drill muttered in disbelief. "Wait, do you really think that's why she's here? Nah, man, she wouldn't do that."

"Wouldn't she?" he said sarcastically. "Either way, I can't take that chance. I need her shares."

"So what are you going to do? Seduce her out of them? Get her to fall in love with you?"

Spencer didn't answer. That's exactly what he had in mind. But he knew he needed more than just seduction. "She needs something that will appeal to her on another level, a professional level. I know she's all about furthering her career."

"Meaning what? You're gonna make her an offer she can't refuse."

"That's exactly what I intend to do. I haven't done an interview in five years. My publicist gets dozens of requests. I'll offer her an exclusive interview with me."

Drill chuckled. "And you think that will work?"

"It'll work. I saw the look in her eyes."

"Did you even ask her why Mason left her the shares?"

"Yes, she said she didn't know."

"You believe her?" he asked.

"I don't know what to believe. Leaving her his shares in his will makes no sense."

"Mason did his own thing, you know that. Maybe he left her the shares to bring you two back together since he was the one who broke you two up."

"He didn't break us up. The book did. She did. I'll

catch you later." Spencer ended the call and looked in the direction of Tia's beach house. He began walking. This wasn't over and it wasn't about what he was feeling for her. This was about his company. She owned Mason's shares of SCE—one third—and that meant she owned a share of his heart.

Chapter 3

If he was surprised to see her, he kept it to himself. But that wasn't surprising. That's how the Spencer Cage rolled. Everything he felt was hidden deep inside. He came across as insensitive to most people. She never knew why he was so closed off, but he was. When she told him she loved him, he didn't respond. She figured it had to do with his upbringing, but since he never talked about his childhood, she could only speculate. In all the time they'd been together, she was never able to touch his heart. She wasn't sure anyone ever could.

Still, seeing him was a shock. She often wondered what she'd do if they ever came face-to-face again. This certainly wasn't how she imagined it. She had hoped to be cool and restrained. But upon seeing Spencer, she knew she was going to fail miserably. The man pushed her buttons and he knew exactly which ones to push. She had mourned the loss for a long time. Getting over him was the hardest thing she had to do. Now, seeing him again brought it all back.

Her heart was still beating wildly when she got back to the cottage. She sat down and shook her head. Seeing Spencer was more than just seeing an old lover. The man stirred everything in her body. His voice, his touch, even a brief glance from him made her want him. The memories of them being together, laughing, talking, making love, swept over her. It was the best time of her life. No man had ever and probably never would affect her the way he did. He made her feel strong and invincible, like she could conquer anything. She missed that. She missed him.

It was obvious the hope of rekindling something with him was impossible. Her heart ached knowing he hated her so much. Maybe he was right. Maybe she should have reconsidered publishing the biography. But where do you draw the line between love and responsibility?

Her cell phone rang. She glanced at the caller ID. It was her good friend and agent, Pamela Gibson. She debated whether to answer the phone knowing Pam would have a dozen questions for her after leaving a cryptic message about refusing an assignment and basically quitting her job. "Hello."

"Natalia, it's Pam. I've been trying to call you for

hours. I got your message. What's going on? Are you okay? Where are you?"

Tia took a deep breath. Hearing a friendly voice was exactly what she needed. "Hi, Pam. I'm fine. I'm in Martha's Vineyard."

"Martha's Vineyard," she said, surprised. "What are you doing there? I thought you were headed to Paris on your next assignment. What happened?"

"I turned down the assignment."

"That's not like you."

"I decided I needed to take a vacation instead."

"A vacation! Since when do you go on vacation?" Pam asked.

"Since never, so I'm definitely due for one right now. I have four months vacation. I'm only taking a month now. I think I just needed some down time. I told Greer I couldn't do the Paris assignment. He didn't take it well."

"I'm sure he didn't."

"I have a feeling you'll be hearing from him soon."

"He's already called me twice. But I wanted to talk with you before talking to him. No worries, I'll take care of him later. But honestly, Tatiana, this isn't like you to just walk away from an assignment. You love what you do. What's going on?"

"To tell you the truth, I'm not sure. I just know I can't do it anymore. Maybe I just need some time away from it all."

"What do you mean?"

"I think I need something different. I don't know what. Maybe journalism isn't what I really want to do anymore."

"Is this about what happened in Istanbul?"

Tia closed her eyes and leaned her head back. Remembering what happened was always too easy. That moment changed everything for her. It was no longer about getting the story at all costs. "I don't know, Pam, maybe, probably. I just know I need a change," she said, feeling a sense of anxiety building up inside of her.

"Understandably. A lot of overseas correspondents burn out. The pressure of the job and the constant threat and human suffering can get to anyone sooner or later."

"It's not just that. For two and a half years I was interviewing heads of state and industry leaders, now I'm assigned puff pieces. After Istanbul that's all they wanted me to do. It's like I'm being punished for being in the right place at the wrong time."

"Truthfully, it's all politics. I'm sure there were more than a few other reporters eager to get to that story. And there you were, right in the center of all the action. And you were incredible."

"It wasn't my fault that the story unfolded right in front of me. I just did what I was trained to do, report the news."

"So, what do you want to do now?" she asked.

"I don't know yet. Something different. Three years is a long time to see the worst of everything, all the misery and suffering. Seeing the devastation up close is heartbreaking."

"Okay, what do you think about writing another book?" Pam said. "I've always said your biography of Mason Brooks was your best work and it was a financial success."

Tia thought about Mason Brooks and what her biography had done to him. It was her first and only book. She couldn't see herself writing another one again. She'd never expected it to change everybody's life so drastically. Her career skyrocketed while his took a downward spiral. "No, I don't think so. But that's why I'm taking some time off. I need to think about what I want to do next. Who knows, maybe I'll start my own news website."

"Yes, I love that idea," Pam said excitedly. "You should."

"I was joking, Pam," Tia said, but then thought about it since Pam got so excited.

"I'm not. You could do it."

Actually the idea didn't sound as far-fetched as she first thought. She knew everything there was to know about covering the news. Maybe she could. "Where am I going to get the money to finance a news website?"

"Didn't you tell me some attorney called you a few times a while back to ask if you were interested in selling your shares in Cage Enterprises?"

"Yeah, he did. But I can't do that, not now, anyway.

There's a stipulation attached to ownership of the shares."

"Still, I think a website like *The Daily Beast* or *The Huffington Post* is a brilliant idea. Why don't you research it? In the meantime, take all the time you need and I'll put out some feelers to see what opportunities are out there and maybe come up with a few suggestions on this end. We'll get you back on track in no time."

"Sounds great. Thanks, Pam, for everything," she said.

"You're welcome. So, Martha's Vineyard? What made you decide to go there?"

Tia looked around happily and hopefully. "My sisters and I rent a cottage from family friends every summer. I don't know how much longer we'll be doing it though. Everything's changing. But I have great summer memories here. And it's the one place in the world where I know I can relax."

"Are you still having problems sleeping?"

"Yes, sometimes. Not as much as before," she said, deciding not to tell her agent that she hadn't really slept in the six weeks since Istanbul. She'd been running on empty for a while, and burnout was catching up fast. She needed sleep. She just couldn't do it. "As soon as my sister gets here I'm gonna eat and sleep for a week."

Just then she saw Spencer walking up the path toward the beach house. Her heart trembled. "Pam, I'll call you in a few days." She pushed the button ending the call and slipped the phone in her pocket again. She stood and walked down the steps and met him halfway.

"I hope I'm not intruding," he said.

"I don't know yet," she said hesitantly.

He nodded. "I deserved that. Look, I had to find you. I'm sorry about all that back there. I couldn't just leave it like that. We meant a lot to each other at one time. I'd like for us to maybe get back to that place. Truce?" he said, extending his hand. She half smiled and nodded as she shook his hand. He reached out with his other hand and touched her cheek then ran his finger down the side of her face. She opened her mouth automatically and a small gasp escaped. She remembered the gentle stroking that set her body afire all too well. And like before, she burned instantly. All it took was just one touch. She raised her chin and averted her gaze.

"You're right. What's in the past is in the past. Neither of us can change what happened," he continued. "So you're in London now. How is it there?" he asked.

"Rainy, foggy, sunny, you know the drill. How's the rest of the world?" she asked.

He half chuckled. "All right, I guess. So, how've you been, Tia?" he asked.

"Good, real good, working hard," she said.

"I saw the piece you did a few weeks ago on that terrorist blast in Istanbul. I was surprised to see you covering that story. It looked pretty bad. I didn't know you did on-camera work."

She nodded and looked away. "I don't usually, and yes, it was a dangerous situation."

"A lot more than dangerous I'd say," he added. "How close were you to the initial blast?"

"I was in a café right across the street when the first bomb went off. Two of the people I was with died. Had I not gotten up to take a phone call to get better reception…" she added, then paused to change the subject. "So what about you, how've you been?" she asked.

"I've been okay," he said, nodding.

She smiled. "I'd say you've been a lot more than just okay. You're everywhere doing everything—music, movies, clothing—you're doing it all. Congratulations. It's what you've always wanted—to rule the world, right?"

"I'm just trying to keep up with you. You look really good. I barely recognized you at first," he said admiringly as his eyes swept leisurely down her body, lingering slowly on her sweet, luscious curves. The purple bikini top and the sweet swell of her breasts was his undoing. The front of his pants tightened as he quickly thought about the rest of her body, the part he didn't readily see. "Mmm, you look good enough to eat," he added seductively as he licked his lips, flashing the single dimple that he knew always made her weak in the knees.

She boldly looked down the front of him. "Right back at you," she said, teasingly. She decided to omit the part where he looked like pure sexual temptation.

"Is that an invitation to feast? Because if it is…" he said, playfully taking a step closer to her. She moved back. He watched as her reaction was immediate. A slow, easy smile tipped his full lips at seeing her smile and the ruby blush flash across her cheeks. He knew what that comment would do to her. He'd bet money that she was already wet for him right now, because he sure as hell was hard for her. His eyes drifted down slowly again lingering on her hips, which he knew so well.

It was obvious he could still make her want him and vice versa. He watched as she took a hesitant step forward and then stop. His body instantly reacted. She was still too damn intoxicating. He took a deep breath as a flood of memories hit him all at once—the first time they met, the first time they kissed, the first time they made love. The sexual passion was explosive every time. They were insatiable. Maybe seeing her again wasn't such a good idea. He was supposed to be seducing her, not the other way around.

"Spencer, what are you doing here? Aren't you supposed to be somewhere else?" she said.

"What makes you say that? Where am I supposed to be?"

"Not here. Don't you have a video shoot in L.A. or something like that?"

Spencer smiled knowingly. His schedule was even more heavily guarded than the gold in Fort Knox. No one knew about his video shoot in L.A. So, for her to know was telling. "The shoot was postponed for two weeks. But the question is, how did you know about it?"

"I'm still a reporter, word gets out," she said simply.

"No, not this word," he assured her. "Have you been keeping tabs on me?" he asked, his full lips spreading into a satisfied smile.

"Why?" she asked.

"You didn't answer my question."

She shook her head. "Don't flatter yourself."

He chuckled, shaking his head. "You still didn't answer my question. Same old Tia," he said, "keeping everything close to the vest." His eyes drifted downward.

"No, not the same old Tia, not anymore," she confirmed, looking down at his bare chest, too. "Not for a very, very long time."

He looked up and arched his brow with interest. "Really, that sounds promising," he challenged.

"As I said, don't flatter yourself. What I meant when I asked if you had someplace else to be is I know you hate places like this, always have. You once told me that you never wanted to come here."

"That was before. I have a house here now," he said.

"You do?" she said in disbelief.

"Yes," he added. "I have the place a few houses down the beach. They call it the Lundy house."

"You mean the Louise Lundy estate?" she asked.

"Yeah, that's the one. I bought it last year as an investment. I started coming here and found I liked it. It's very private and secluded."

She was impressed. The Sullivan's home was quaint and lovely, one of the few remaining older homes on the south shore of the island. But the Lundy estate was a breathtaking showplace. There was no other place like it. It was spectacular. "Wow, impressive. I remember the Lundy estate from when I used to summer here years ago."

"It's big, but it's also very comfortable," he said, staring at her. "Have you ever been inside?"

"No."

"Why don't you come over? I'll give you a tour."

"No, no, thanks. That's okay, maybe another time," she said.

He looked behind her. "This is where you're staying?"

She nodded. "The Sullivan's cottage, they're friends of my family. As a matter of fact the owners are on a cruise with my parents now. We used to come up and stay here when I was growing up. Now my sisters and I rent the cottage every summer."

"Are your sisters here, too?"

"No."

"You're alone?" he asked.

She nodded.

"So are you coming or going?"

"I don't know yet. I just got here a few hours ago, but…"

"Are you thinking about leaving the island because of me? Because if you are…"

"Still conceited as ever I see," she said shaking her head slowly. "No Spencer Cage, not everything is about you. My sister, Niki, won't be able to join me for a few days. I'm thinking of just going to visit her in Key West instead. But then again," she paused, "maybe not. So, as you can see, none of this has anything to do with you."

"I've missed that. Nobody tells the no-holds-barred truth like you, right?" he said, then realized from her expression that she'd taken what he'd said as an insult. "That wasn't meant as an insult," he said. "I hope you decide to stay. Three years is a long time. We should catch up."

"Maybe that's not such a good idea," she said. "Maybe it's best if we keep our distance while we're here."

"Why?" he said.

"Does the adage 'oil and water don't mix' mean anything to you? Besides this is a working vacation for me."

"Is there a terrorist attack here on the island I don't know about?" he said facetiously.

She smiled at his silliness. "No. But I'm thinking about making some life-changing decisions."

"You mean giving up London and being a foreign correspondent?"

"I don't know yet, maybe," she said evasively then turned away anxiously.

He wanted to know more, but he knew she was done.

"Okay, it was really nice seeing you again," he added. She nodded as she took a step back, turned and started walking back to the beach cottage.

His eyes slowly drifted down the length of her body as she walked away. She looked exactly the same, breathtaking. He could feel the uncomfortable bulge between his legs get even harder. She always did this to him. "Hey, what are you doing later tonight?" he called out.

She stopped and turned. "I'm still on London time, so hopefully sleeping. Why?"

"I have a proposition for you."

"A proposition? What kind of proposition?" she asked.

"Stop by the club tonight, we'll talk."

"The club?" she said curiously.

"The Cage, it's in Edgartown. There's a private birthday party for me tonight."

She smiled. "That's right. Your birthday is coming up soon. Happy birthday!"

He shook his head. "Stop by and wish me a happy birthday tonight," he urged.

"Since when do you ever go to your own parties?"

"I just might this time," he said.

She shook her head and started walking backward. "Either way, I don't think that would be a good idea."

"I do. It's small and private. Think about it," he shouted, "and then come anyway."

She smiled wide but gave no definitive answer. She

waved before turning around again. When she got back inside she locked the French doors and went straight up to her room and closed the door. Looking around, the first thing she saw were her bags sitting on the floor where she'd left them. She hadn't unpacked. It would be so easy to grab her bags, take the ferry and head back to Cape Cod. The thought had crossed her mind several times. But she knew she wouldn't. It was too late to catch the ferry. And besides, she knew she had unfinished business here. She needed to get her life settled, and finding closure with Spencer was the first step to moving on.

She knew Spencer well and she was no fool. Seeing him on the beach was a surprise, but seeking her out was strategic on his part. He was an excellent chess player and businessman. He had street smarts and was far more intelligent than some gave him credit for. Underestimating him was not the issue for her, she knew him too well.

He was cunning and calculating. He never did anything without an ulterior motive. For him, there was always an end game. So every instinct in her body told her he wanted something from her. It seemed a simple afterthought, but she knew better. There was a reason he stopped by to invite her to the party tonight. He wanted something and she had just enough time on her hands to find out what it was. So she decided to play his game.

There was no way her heart was in any danger. She'd done her time with Spencer already. She may have wanted his body, sure, but that's all. She walked over to the window and looked out. He was gone. It was becoming dark already, yet she felt energized. She went down to the kitchen and found some take out menus at one of the few seafood places in the Vineyard that delivered.

After placing her order, she hung up the rest of her clothes. When the food came she ate out on the back porch, enjoying the view. The notion of attending Spencer's birthday party was tempting. She knew he'd come late. He always did. He'd make a ten minute appearance then leave and that was fine with her.

If he indeed wanted something from her, then she was going to make him work for it. The answer came almost instantly, why not? He was the perfect man to flush her pipes. She smiled and chuckled to herself as she went upstairs to shower and get dressed.

Chapter 4

Spencer went back down the steps and walked along the beach toward his house. When he got close, he just stood looking out at the waves, lost in his memories. Seeing Tia had unnerved him more than he'd expected. It brought everything back. No woman in the world could ever do what she did to him. With a single glance, she made him burn inside and out. He shook his head. Yeah, seeing Tia had thrown him for a loop.

He was always in control. Nothing and no one had ever gotten to him, except her. She had gotten to him then, and she was getting to him now. He turned and headed toward his house. Drill was standing on the terrace when he approached. "Hey," Spence said.

"Now let me guess what took so long. You went to see Tia."

"Yeah," Spencer said, walking across the terrace to the sliding glass door. Drill followed.

"So you ask her about buying her shares?"

"No, but I invited her to the party tonight."

"A'ight, I'll put her name on the list," Drill said as he closed the glass doors once they were inside.

"Don't bother, she's not coming."

Drill smiled. "Five hundred says you're wrong. She'll be there."

"You usually play the long shots, not the impossible runs. I don't want to take your money." They headed to the kitchen. Spencer grabbed a bottle of water and tossed one to Drill.

"Five hundred's on the table, you in or what?" Drill said as he caught the bottle, twisted the cap off and tossed it into the trashcan from across the room like a basketball in a hoop.

"A'ight, I got you covered, but it's a sucker bet," Spencer warned, and then mimicked Drill's shot, except he missed the trashcan. He walked over, picked up the cap and dropped it in. "Tia and I are long over. She's not coming. Partying never was her thing."

Drill chuckled after taking a long swig of water. "Yeah, right, she'll be there. Mark my words, that woman's gonna be in your blood forever."

"You're wrong," Spencer said leaving the kitchen.

"Yeah, whatever," Drill said, following but stopping when they came to the front door. "Look, I gotta get to the club and make sure everything's straight for tonight. You all right with all this?"

"Yeah, I'm fine, go."

"A'ight, I'll check you later."

They shoulder bumped. Drill opened the door to leave, but then turned back just as Spencer started toward the studio. "You want a car to pick you up?"

"No, I'll drive. See you there."

"Yeah, and bring my five hundred with you when you come."

Spencer laughed as Drill closed the front door. His phone rang again as he headed to the studio. He didn't answer. He didn't feel like dealing with anyone right now. Basically, he was still in a daze. It wasn't just seeing her, he was surprised by his own reaction to her. He realized that he still had feelings for her. Thankfully he could control them.

He walked into the studio and looked around. Drill had left everything exactly as he asked. The tracks he'd been working on were up and already mixed and ready for his approval. But he didn't feel like hearing them right now. He cleared the board to start something new. All of a sudden he was consumed and totally focused.

For the last five years he had stepped away from his own music to produce other artists and launch his own record label. Success was an understatement. He had far exceeded his own dreams. He had produced the music for megastars around the world. To attach his name to a project was to guarantee platinum sales and millions of dollars. So going back to the recording studio and doing his own music didn't really appeal to him anymore, until now. The last CD he released was for her. Now this one was because of her.

He'd worked steadily on the tracks without stopping. Time passed quickly. Not surprisingly every note flowed, every melody was effortless. Every lyric he wrote was perfection. He couldn't miss even if he tried. Being around Tia always did that to him. She was his Muse—always had been and always would be. Seeing her brought everything back and those same memories were getting to him again.

He smiled at a private joke. "Under the Top" was going to be the title of his first single, as he remembered Tia's bikini. The song was slow and sexy with just enough heat to melt a polar ice cap. The beat was sultry and seductive and pulsed with desire and passion. It was everything he felt when he saw Tia in the purple bikini top. He envisioned the cover art in varying shades of reds, violets, magentas, deep lavender and blues. The video would be a wash of iridescent blue gradating to a vibrant purple just like her bikini top.

Five hours later, Spencer stood in the large shower stall as a stream of cool water cascaded down the front of his chest. He took a deep breath and increased the water pressure. He turned a second knob, and instantly five more strategically placed shower heads and jets vigorously pelted streams of water over the rest of his body. He spread his arms wide placing his hands on the cold marble tile walls. The pulsating jets were exactly what he needed to right now. He didn't want to imagine what the party at the club was going to be like.

Without much provocation the purple bikini top flashed through his mind. His body stiffened. He was hard all over again. She did this to him. Just thinking about her made his juices surge to near explosive arousal. He reached over and turned the water to ice cold. Then he closed his eyes and tilted his face directly in the path of the spray of water.

He thought he was over her. But seeing her brought everything back. She was the itch he couldn't scratch. "My Itch" was the next track he was going to work on, he decided. The beat was fierce with a heavy bass and a Latin rhythm. It was Tia.

Just as quickly he felt the searing pain of an open wound. She had hurt him, betrayed him and then just walked away. But he also felt a raging desire. He wanted her. His body craved her. And just like before, he knew he was going to do any and everything in his power to have her. But this time it was going to be different. It was physical, yes, but it was also personal. They had unfinished business and now that she was back, he intended to settle it.

After another ten minutes of the watery assault he opened his eyes, grabbed the nozzles and turned off the water. As soon as he did, he heard it. The phone was ringing again. It was his personal line. He knew exactly who it was. His crew was already at the party.

Everyone was there, all waiting for him to arrive. But he really wasn't in the mood.

"Damn," he muttered as he got out of the shower still aroused. Just the thought of her had gotten him like this. Drill was right, time and distance didn't matter, she would always be in his heart. He grabbed a towel and quickly ran it over his hard body. He glanced at his naked profile in the mirror. Dark, nearly black eyes stared back. He was tired and frustrated and he knew exactly what he needed. It had been a long time, too damn long.

There had been plenty of offers, ever since he was fourteen years old. But he had had his fill of groupies, gold diggers and hangers-on. He wanted something real. He wanted the one woman that had gotten to him. He wanted Tatiana Coles. He tossed the damp towel at his reflection and walked back into his bedroom and restlessly looked around. He wanted to skip the party and go to see Tia instead.

He grabbed and put on a pair of dark slacks and a white shirt then walked back out into his bedroom.

Tonight was another birthday party. It was his third celebration and it wasn't even his birthday yet. This one was being thrown by his crew from the old neighborhood. That meant he had to attend. He walked over to the massive floor-to-ceiling bay windows and looked down at the back terrace, then out across the horizon. The stunning scenic beauty of the Atlantic Ocean and the massive black sky was breathtaking. Buying this house was a brilliant idea.

The house phone rang again. He glanced over with no intention of answering. He grabbed his cell and headed downstairs. Maybe this was exactly what he needed. He'd been bombarded all morning and afternoon with phone calls from industry people and reporters. They all wanted the same thing—an interview or, at the very least, information. Neither of which he intended to give. The word was out, something big was happening at Cage Enterprises and everyone wanted to know what it was.

Ironic as it sounded now, at one point in his career he wouldn't hesitate to give an interview and get free publicity. He even coveted it. The more people knew about his music the better. But that was before. Now he'd gone reclusive and the answer was always 'no comment' and that seemed to make them want him even more.

Still it was a game and all part of the business he loved. And in his business, publicity was all that mattered. If people weren't talking about you that meant you were no longer relevant. And that meant your career was over. But now the last thing he wanted to deal with was people in his business.

His cell phone rang this time. It was Drill, he answered.

"Yo, man, where you at? You still in the studio?" Drill said.

"Nah, I'm done for the night."

"So you comin' down here or what? The party's jumpin'."

"Nah, I've got something I need to take care of tonight," Spencer said, intending to go to Tia.

"Are you sure?" Drill said.

"Yeah, why?"

"Because you need to be getting up off the cash."

"What are you talking about?"

"Five hundred dollars."

"What?"

"Tatiana Coles is here."

"She came?" he said completely astonished.

"Yep, Donavan's got her all locked up though. As soon as she walked in, he was on her hard. You know the lover's trying to make his play. He's always had an itch for her. She was his forbidden fruit, the one he couldn't have, so I guess he figures it's his turn to get with her now."

"Damn, a'ight. I'm on my way now."

"A'ight, see you in a bit."

The definition of 'a bit' was exactly fourteen minutes and three seconds. Speeding had always been his vice. He drove up to the popular Cage club. A crowd of people stood out front hoping to see someone famous or get inside even though the party was by invitation only. He pulled up and barely parked the car before jumping out and hurrying inside through the private entrance. He waved as his name was repeatedly shouted and cell phone cameras immediately began taking his picture.

He continued up to the second level, and then quickly cut through the office to the large balcony overlooking the club.

The scene was outrageous. There was a sea of people dancing. The office and his private wing were designed to be as close to soundproof as possible. But as soon as he opened the sliding glass door, he was assaulted by the sound of pounding music. He stepped out onto the balcony and looked down. There was an immediate cheer as a number of guests looked up and saw him. They waved and called his name. He smiled, nodded and waved back. There was another loud roar of applause. His cell rang. It was Drill again. "Yo, 'bout time."

"Everything cool?" Spencer asked.

"Yeah, I had to dismiss a few fools, but it's all good."

"Okay," Spencer said impatiently. "Where are you?"

"I just walked outside. I'm headed to the DJ booth," Drill said. "Where you at?" he added.

"Upstairs on the balcony," Spencer said stepping out farther onto the balcony and waving his hand. There was another wave of cheers and applause. He didn't even notice it this time. The only thing he focused on was looking for Tia and Donavan.

He knew Donavan too well. He was arrogant, with an attitude of entitlement when it came to women and what he wanted. He was singularly focused on power and sex. If a woman didn't respond to his advances, he had no problem finding a way around it. Alcohol, drugs or pills, he didn't really care as long as he got what he wanted. A sudden anger spiked in Spencer. He had no idea how long she'd been here, but he knew Donavan wasn't a particularly patient man when he wanted something or someone.

"Where are they?" Spencer demanded next.

"Donavan and Tia, last I saw, they were in the club inside by the dance floor," Drill said. Spencer tensed. He spotted Drill standing and looking around near the outside DJ booth. "No, I see them. There they are, by the pergola on the lower level dance floor," Drill said. A second later Spencer saw them, too. Tia had her back to him and Donavan was looking right up at him. He placed his hand on Tia's arm and steered her away.

An instant feeling of possessiveness shot through Spencer. Donavan was the self-professed lover in their crew. He often said that women flocked to him like a sale at the shopping mall. To Donavan this was just a game, a competition to prove he could get anything Spencer had, including his company and Tia. He often went after his ex's, just to prove that he could get them.

"So, you coming down or staying up there all night?"

"I'm on my way," he said. *Tia and Donavan*—before the idea settled in his mind he was already out the door. Moments later he made his appearance. A few minutes after that, he was headed out to the terrace in the back of the club.

Getting through the rush of fans, friends and admirers was difficult. Everyone wanted to see him or speak to him. He finally made it to the terrace outside the club.

Applause rang out once more. He nodded and waved while accepting handshakes, hugs and fist bumps. As usual, women attached themselves to him, most were half dressed and hung on to him like with a vise grip, all vying for his undivided attention. Several even kissed him. But he couldn't be bothered. He was too busy focusing on finding Tia.

He stood on the top step and scanned the crowd again. The crush of guests was crazy. Then he spotted Tia. Donavan was right beside her. Donavan said something to get her attention. She turned looking directly at him. Spencer immediately started in her direction.

Three minutes later he had effectively pushed through the crowd. A few feet away he saw Tia and Donavan still engaged in conversation. He was standing too close and nearly whispering in her ear. She nodded while looking around casually. He knew the look, she wanted out. Then she glanced around and spotted him approaching. She smiled and lit up his world. She said something because Donavan turned around looking especially peeved.

Chapter 5

Tia arrived at The Cage nightclub later than she'd expected. As soon as she got out of the cab she heard the music. She went to the front door, was asked her name and then was admitted. The inside was very chic and stylish. The main area had a large dance floor and two bars, but also an outside terrace area with a beautiful view of the ocean. The music was loud and the place was packed. The private party she expected was anything but. There had to be at least two hundred guests there already. She saw television and movie stars mingling with politicians, sports and music celebrities. Everybody who was anybody and vacationing in Martha's Vineyard was there.

She mingled a while. There were a few people she knew from visiting Martha's Vineyard over the years.

Since it was a small summer resort island, at some point everyone knew or knew of everyone else. As acquaintances and old friends, they talked easily, catching up and reminiscing about hanging out years ago.

She also saw a few people she'd known from her days with Spencer, Mason and BoomBox Productions. Some spoke, others didn't. Apparently to some she was persona non grata. Spencer's crew was there of course. Drill made a point of speaking to her. They had always had a comfortable, friendly relationship. Even after everything that went down between her, Mason and Spencer he was cool with her. They even kept in touch over the years. They talked a few minutes until Donavan intervened.

Donavan was different than Spencer's other friends. He took a lot of getting used to. She never spent this much time with him before. But as expected, he was exactly as she'd heard—an obnoxious womanizer who preyed on Spencer's leftovers. Apparently she was now in that category. She had managed to get away from him a few times, but he always managed to find her and start his pursuit all over again. Tall and handsome, she could easily see how some women found him attractive. But he definitely wasn't her style. Still he insisted on staying by her side the whole evening.

"So, I hear you live in London," he said.

"Yes, most of the time, but I travel a lot."

"How long have you been there?"

"Three years," she said, knowing he knew exactly how long she'd lived in London.

"Yeah, that's right. You moved there right after that book was released, right?" He started laughing. "So, you still write those tell-all biographies of celebs?"

"No, Mason was my first and last."

"I have an idea, why don't you write my biography? I have money, fame, power, and I've got the number one hit rap song out. See these people, they love me. And I'll let you in on a little secret. I'm just about to take over and have it all."

"Take over and have what?" she asked curiously.

"What else…?" he said cryptically with a sly, suggestive smile.

She shook her head. "Sorry, I don't write books anymore. I'm a foreign correspondent."

"That's right I saw you on television. I didn't know you were a TV reporter."

"I'm not. I write news stories and do interviews. Istanbul was an exception."

"See you should do another book, 'cause that number you did on Mason was on the money. No denying, you had his shit down cold. I loved it. Seriously, who was your source, Spencer?" he asked. Tia just smiled and looked around the room. "Come on, you can tell me. I won't tell anyone, I promise." He inched closer. "It was Spencer, right?" She still didn't answer. "A'ight, be like that." He started laughing again. "Look, I'm not saying Mason was right or wrong with what he did. He just thought he had it all figured out. Still, you did a number on him."

"Actually, I did my job objectively. Everything I wrote was the truth."

"Yeah, but still, that shit was rough. Mason was pissed when it came out. You know he blamed Spencer."

She looked at him. She didn't know. "Why would he blame Spencer? He had nothing to do with it."

"I guess he figured Spencer told you all that stuff. But, yeah, they didn't speak for a long time after that. Shit was fierce for a minute."

She looked at him questioning. "What do you mean?" she asked. He looked at her. His gaze was cold and serious. She didn't need him to answer. She knew exactly what he meant. "So what happened?" she continued.

"Drill stepped in and Mason calmed down. I was surprised. He was cool about it after a while. Even after the feds indicted him on tax fraud, he was cool with Spencer. But for real, I don't know why. Personally, I would have kicked Spencer's sorry ass if he turned on me like that."

Her reporter instincts came out instantly. She was a listener and people liked to talk around her. She couldn't help what they said. They always seemed to open up. She read people easily and by asking just a few questions, she usually got exactly what she wanted. "I thought Spencer was your boy. You all grew up together, right?"

"Nah, nah, hell, no. I didn't grow up in no hood with the rest of them. That was Drill and Riley. I grew up in

Boston. My peeps got bank. So I got deep pockets on my own. I don't need his bank, never did."

"Really. So you don't really know much about him, either?"

"Hell, no, nobody does. I doubt even Drill knows the real deal on Spencer. He keeps his shit close."

There was applause. Everyone turned around and looked up. She saw that Spencer had stepped out onto the balcony and looked around. "There's your man," Donavan whispered right in her ear. "Oh, but I guess not anymore." He was too close.

"No, not anymore," she said.

"Yeah, what happened with all that? Ya'll was thick for a while. I heard he was even talking marriage."

"Like I said, not anymore."

"So check this out, I heard Mason left you his shares in Spencer's company and you're thinking about selling."

"Is that what you heard?" she said, neither denying nor confirming his statement.

"Yeah, so is it true?"

"Why do you ask?"

"If it's true, then I might be interested in making you a business offer."

"What kind of offer?" she asked curiously, but knowing there was no way she'd go for it, whatever it was.

"I'd be interested in taking the shares off your hands for a very lucrative return. I can also make it worth your while in other ways." He leered.

"Donavan…"

"Look, I know Mason would want you to do what's best for the company. Right now that's me. So why don't I have my attorney call you and we can do some serious business together. His name's Portman."

"I think you heard wrong." There was another round of applause. She turned around to see what was going on.

"See you playing now. Okay, that's a'ight. I got time. I always get exactly what I want in the end."

She turned back to him, "Was that a threat?"

He laughed. "Nah, baby, that was the truth. I'm a lover not a fighter."

"So when did you two actually meet?" she asked after the applause died down again.

"Spencer and me, I met him in college. I was a senior, he was a sophomore. He was the golden-boy even back then. Everybody loved his ass. Shit, the women damn near fell at his feet when he walked in a room," he said, gnashing and gritting his teeth. His jaw tightened and she watched his facial muscles tense. "But you already know about all that, don't you. You were one of them," he said, looking at her slyly.

"That was a long time ago."

"Yeah," he started chuckling. "You messed the man up big time. He was trippin' out after that book."

"Really."

"Oh, yeah, Spencer was pissed. Hell, I think he was more pissed than Mason. Girl, you know you broke that man's heart when you walked out on him. You had him whipped. I thought I'd never see a woman do that to him. But I'm not like that," he said then hit his chest Neanderthal-like. "Real men don't drop that shit like that. But see I know that's why you and Spencer broke up. You know he blamed you for that stuff that happened with Mason and BoomBox Productions."

"You think so," she said unfazed, not really needing his confirmation. She knew in her heart he was furious with her about the book even though she was sure he knew it was all true. He asked her not to send it in to the publisher, but she did anyway. She had no choice.

"Hell, I know so. Don't you know he wants what you got?"

"What do I have?" she asked not sure what he was talking about.

"Now you're just being funny. Seriously, I'll make it worth your while," Donavan said, and then turned his attention to a passing waiter. "Yo, my man, can a brotha get another drink over here?" The waiter came quickly and offered champagne. "Nah, I'm talkin' 'bout some black Jack. Go get me a real drink, a man's drink. And bring one for the lady here," he ordered.

She knew the interview was over and he knew he'd said too much. She looked around, seeing that Spencer had finally arrived at his party. By the time Donavan's drinks arrived, Spencer was walking toward them. Donavan handed her one of the drinks as he approached.

She smiled and shook her head. His supercool swagger was unmistakable. "Here's the man of honor," she said.

Donavan turned and smiled, but it wasn't genuine. She suspected Spencer knew it, too. The two men shook hands and bumped shoulders and greeted each other cordially. Spencer never took his eyes from her face. "So the big man has finally graced us with his presence," Donavan snarled. "I was wondering when your ass was gonna show up. You know we need to talk about that thing."

"Not now," Spencer said, still focusing his attention solely on Tia. Neither spoke or acknowledged the other. They just stared and half smiled.

"So, I guess you see who's here with me tonight while you were up in the studio. Tatiana came all the way from London to be here with me tonight. She and I are having a little private conversation," Donavan said, smirking and moving closer to Tia for added confirmation. "So if you'll excuse us." Spencer didn't respond.

"I'm glad you decided to come," Spencer said to Tia.

"Thanks."

"Wait, you knew she was coming here tonight?" Donavan said stepping aside and looking at Tia.

"Of course, he invited me," Tia said smiling.

"Oh, so it's like that. I thought ya'll was done."

"We're just friends," Tia said.

"A'ight, I'm gonna get another drink. Portman will be calling you," Donavan said directly to Tia. Spencer ignored him, still focusing on Tia. Donavan walked away. He looked back. He was obviously pissed.

"Portman, Donavan's attorney? What was all that about?"

"Nothing important," she said dismissively.

An icy chill shot through him. He would bet that the nothing important was Donavan making his move. He also knew he needed to take control of this now. It was time to make his move, too. "You look stunning tonight," Spencer said letting his eyes slowly drift down her body, easing along the curvy halter dress she'd worn. It fit her perfectly, showing just enough cleavage to be alluring and just enough skin to be enticing.

"Aww, just stunning? You mean I'm no longer edible," she teased, mocking his earlier remark on the beach.

He licked his lips as his eyes grew more intense. Her stomach trembled. "Sweetheart, that goes without saying," he assured her. Then moments passed as neither spoke. They just stared at each other.

"So, are we going to just stare at each other all night?"

"No," he said. "Come, let's dance." He took the drink from her hand and guided her to the dance floor just as a slow song began playing. When they got to the center he turned and smiled, then eased his hand around her waist. She stepped closer, placing her hand on his shoulder. Being this close, feeling his body, smelling his scent, was wreaking havoc on her nerves and her body. Then they began to move to the slow seductive melody.

Unlike other couples dancing around them, who ground and gyrated, they danced leaving a sliver of space between them. Polite and courteous, they held each other with respectful restraint. Then their gazes connected, still neither spoke. Everything about the moment seemed too perfect for words. Slowly but surely the world faded away, leaving only them.

Then, gradually, as if by some unknown force, they moved closer. The polite, platonic positioning gave way to desperate longing. He took her hand in his and began rubbing his thumb in her palm. The silky, sensuous feel of his gentle touch made her stomach quiver. It was arousing and erotic. Yet at the same time it was caring and innocent. He intertwined their fingers and kissed her hand tenderly. She watched him, holding her breath as her heart thundered in her chest.

Spencer wrapped his arms around her waist and Tia wrapped her arms around his neck. She held tight and inhaled deeply as she closed her eyes, enjoying the feel of being held by the man she once loved with all her heart. His hand, with fingers spread wide, slowly slid up and down her bare back. His caress was intoxicating. He gripped her tighter. She exhaled and relaxed against the hard firmness of his body.

Chest to chest, pelvis to pelvis, they were in their own world now. As the music played, their embrace grew even closer. She laid her head on his shoulder and neck. His hands held her even tighter. "Stay with me tonight," he whispered close. The warmth of his breath sent a shimmer of excitement down her neck. "One night only, no ties, no commitments."

She leaned back and looked up at him. He was serious. She shook her head. "You know that's not a good idea."

"Are you sure?"

"Yeah, I'm sure."

Suddenly the music changed. The DJ played one of Spencer's old songs. The beat was fast and pulsating. The guests were instantly excited. The noise level spiked to a near-earsplitting decibel as everyone on the dance floor started jumping, rapping and yelling. Arms waved in the air and the thunderous beat reverberated around them. "I hope you're enjoying yourself," he said. She frowned and shook her head moving closer to hear what he said. "I said I hope you're enjoying yourself?" he repeated louder.

She nodded her head. "Yes, I am. Sorry, I can barely hear you."

"Come on. Let's go over here," he said. He guided her away from the main dance floor. They kept walking, coming to the end of the paved area and stopped at a decorative railing just off the beach. There were other couples already walking around the shoreline. "Is this better?"

"Yes, much better, thanks. Sorry about that," she

said looking back at the party still going on. "I guess I'm not used to the loud speakers anymore."

"You never were."

"No, I guess not. So, happy birthday," she said then leaned in and sweetly kissed his cheek. He held her in place a few seconds longer. She inhaled the spicy scent of his cologne. A rush of excitement swept through her.

"It's in another few days, but I guess you won't be here then, or will you?"

"Actually, I've decided to hang around and wait for Niki."

He smiled happily. "Good, I'm glad to hear that. And I think that deserves some champagne." He spotted a waiter and motioned to him. He quickly approached with a silver tray of flutes. Spencer picked up two glasses of champagne and handed her one.

"Thank you, but I think I've had my two drink quota already, especially being jet-lagged. I'm already a little woozy."

"Don't worry. You know I'll take care of you."

She looked up into his eyes then quickly looked away breaking the intense pull she was beginning to feel. It was time to go. "Still, all good things…"

"To memories," he interrupted, raising his glass to toast.

She nodded. "To memories." They each took a sip then looked into each other's eyes over the rim. The burn of desire was surging. "You got here just in time.

I was on my way out. Thank you for inviting me. I had a great time."

"Wait, you're not leaving are you?" he asked, taking her elbow to continue guiding her away from the party. It got quieter and quieter as they walked.

"It's late. I've been here for the last two hours, even if the man of honor wasn't. So, I'm tired. I need to go to bed."

"I have two bedrooms right here in the club."

"Neither of which are mine," she sat the glass down.

"Tia, stay, please." He held her hand to stop her from walking away. "I need to see you. We need to talk."

"Spencer, this isn't going where you think it's going," she said as her heart pounded like a jackhammer. Even as the words left her mouth she knew different. "It was good to see you." She eased her hand away and took a step back.

"You came here for a reason," he interjected quickly.

"Yes, to say happy birthday," she confessed.

"Is that all?" he asked. She nodded. He knew she was lying. "No, come on, you and I go too far back to play games."

She hesitated a moment then nodded. "Agreed, and I'm not interested in going back there again. I came this evening hoping for closure and to hopefully be friends again if we can."

"We are friends," he confirmed with ease.

"Good, I'm glad," she said pulling away.

"I missed you. Three years is a long time to have an itch."

She knew exactly what he was saying. It was the same itch she had had all these years. She looked into his eyes and was instantly lost in desire. He spoke to her without opening his mouth. She suddenly felt the weight of his body pressed against hers, delving deep inside of hers. She shuddered. Intense and forceful, the feeling was irresistible. She wanted to touch him, to be with him. "I'm sure they lined up to help you with your itch."

"Yeah, they lined up, but they weren't what I wanted."

Her nerve endings tingled. This conversation was getting too intense. "We can't always have what we want, can we?" she said.

"Sometimes we can," he said quickly.

"Spencer…"

"Come here," he said quietly as he sat down on the rail.

She didn't move. "Spencer, you're gonna have to get someone else to scratch your itch tonight." She glanced back at the party. The revelers were enjoying themselves. "I'm sure a few of the young women here would love to help you out."

"No one else can, for either of us. Or don't you remember."

She took a deep breath. "I remember." She swallowed hard. She remembered too well. "But that's not me anymore."

"We were good together."

"That was a long time ago," she said. "It's over now."

"Are you sure?" he asked.

She didn't reply.

"I'm here for the next two weeks," he said. "I assume you are, too."

She nodded.

"I suggest we make them memorable."

"Memorable as in sexual?" she said.

"Same as before—no ties, no commitments, no drama. Making love was never a problem for us. We excelled at sexual." He said watching her closely.

She walked over to stand beside him. "But we let it turn into something else."

"We know better."

"Do we?" she questioned, looking over at him.

He looked over at her. "Tia," he said and held her hand again. "We both know why you came here tonight. It's the same reason I was on my way to see you before Drill called me and told me you were here. It's the same reason we were together before and right now. The attraction between us, the chemistry we have is…" he stopped and took a deep breath.

"Addictive," she said.

"Yeah, addictive. So are we going to do memorable?"

"Spencer, don't…"

"Tia, don't listen to your head, listen to your body." Bad advice, her body was on fire and he knew it. She looked away quickly. She hated how he read her so easily. Especially since she couldn't read him at all. She turned to him and half smiled in a way that he knew exactly what she was thinking. The man worked her like a full-time job with overtime pay. "You want to make love, I'm right here for you."

She shook her head. "It can't be you."

"What do you mean? Why can't it be me?" he asked.

She shook her head, "I have to go."

"Wait a minute. How'd you get here?"

"I took a cab."

"Let me drive you home."

"No, it's your party, you need to stay and enjoy it." She leaned in and kissed his lips chaste and tenderly. "Good night. Happy birthday." She tried to move away, but he held tight to her hand. He wrapped his arms around her body and pulled her close. Their mouths hovered a scant second, and then before she knew it she was there in that place where her dreams came true. She kissed him. Lord, she forgot what it was like to have your world completely rocked with a single touch.

She pulled back suddenly. "No, this can't happen—it shouldn't have happened. I shouldn't have done that."

"Says who?" he whispered and leaned in. She held her breath knowing exactly what he was going to do. He reached out and gently cupped her neck drawing her close. Then he slowly captured her mouth. She moaned instantly as the tender kiss deepened. She melted against his body. Her heartbeat quickened.

The man kissed like he invented the technique. His

tongue pressed to her mouth and she opened to him. He immediately delved deeper into her mouth as her body relaxed against his. She moaned as she felt a quiver rush through her. He was opening her up again. Her heart raced and her skin tingled. His taste was her nectar and she imbibed with ravenous hunger. He fed her and she greedily indulged. He was doing things to her—things she'd forgotten were even possible. She felt a wave of pleasure coming on and adjusted her body to absorb the crest. He held her hips and pressed her to his hardness. His gyrations brought on another wave, this time with more intensity. It was harder this time. Still the kiss continued. Time slipped into oblivion.

It was orgasmic foreplay—out in the open for all to witness. She was scandalous, but she didn't care. Passion rocked them and the kiss affirmed it over and over again. She felt another wave surging again. She stilled her body to withstand its awesome force. Hardness pressed against her body. She leaned back, suddenly aware that she was standing between his legs, realizing that the hardness she felt was Spencer. They were breathless, desperate and throbbing with passion. The look of desire in her eyes was reflected in his. "Let's go upstairs."

Her body shook as some semblance of reason, perched precariously on the very edge of insanity, began to take hold. It took everything she had to regain control and to utter the words she knew she had to. "Good night, Spencer." She backed up and quickly walked away.

Spencer watched her go, knowing this wasn't the end of it.

Moments later Donavan walked over smiling like he'd just swallowed a canary. "I guess she wasn't interested, huh?"

Spencer looked at him. "What?"

Donavan tipped his head in the general direction Tia had gone. "Looks like it's over between you two. Maybe you're no longer the man you once were," he taunted.

Spencer smiled slowly. "See that's where you're wrong. It's not over, it's called foreplay." He finished his glass of champagne and nodded to Donavan. "Have a nice evening."

Chapter 6

The cab stand was right outside the club's entrance. Tia hurried over, got in and quickly gave her address to the driver. She noticed the driver glance up at her in his rearview mirror. He repeated the address. She nodded and he drove off. Twenty-five minutes later she was back in the safe security of the Sullivan's cottage.

She went directly to the kitchen and poured herself a tall, ice-cold glass of water and gulped it down. The sudden chill helped, but not enough. She needed relief. She grabbed her cell phone to call her sister, but instantly decided against it. She wasn't ready to let anyone know what was going on. She opened the French doors and stepped outside onto the porch. The night sky was dark, voluminous and filled with a billion sparkling lights. If wishing on a star could give her what she wanted she'd do it, but she knew better. Still…

"Star light, star bright, first star I see tonight, what in the world am I doing here?" She looked around and then chuckled to herself. Okay now she was officially crazy. Maybe jetlag had finally overwhelmed her. She went back into the house, locked the French doors, closed the drapes and headed up the stairs. On the first step the doorbell rang. She went over peeked through the hole and shook her head. A second later she opened the door half smiling.

Spencer was leaning against the door frame smiling all sexy and self-assured. She noticed he had one hand behind his back. She eyed him suspiciously as the gleeful sparkle in his eyes shone. The man ate at her very heart. "What are you doing here, Spencer? You can't be here."

"Would you believe I couldn't stop thinking about you?"

"Stop tempting me," she said.

He smiled and nodded. "Stop tempting me. I like that. Sounds like the perfect song lyric."

"Take it, it's yours."

"Thanks, I just might."

"Good night," she said, attempting to close the door.

"Okay, okay. How about I if I said I couldn't stop thinking about you and I came to apologize."

"Apologize for what?" she asked.

"For tonight. I didn't expect you to come," he said.

"Neither did I, it was a mistake."

"No, don't say that. It felt good being with you again."

"Spencer, there's too much between us to pretend it's all water under the bridge. Our history goes too deep and I have enough drama going on in my life right now."

"What's going on in your life?" he asked.

She shook her head. "It's not about that. This is about you and me and us being here together."

He smirked. "So you're saying this island isn't big enough for the two of us."

"Yeah, something like that," she said, half smiling. He nodded and looked away. "Good night, Spencer. Goodbye." She tried to close the door a second time.

"How about if I said I couldn't stop thinking about you, I came to apologize and I picked up your favorite ice cream," he said quickly before the door closed, moving his hand and showing her the two ice cream cones he'd been holding onto behind his back. His hand was covered with French vanilla ice cream.

Tia laughed. "Oh, my God, are you crazy? It's four o'clock in the morning. Where in the world did you get ice cream cones at this hour of the morning?"

"One of the homemade ice cream parlors in town sent a few dozen large containers to the party."

"Look at you, you're a mess," she said, still laughing at the sight of his hand covered in melted cream.

"Are you going to help me out here or just stand there laughing at me?" he said, offering one of the vanilla cones to her. She took it gingerly. The dripping cone immediately began melting on her hand. She licked it then held the door wider for him to enter. "Come in and get cleaned up."

"Do you have any idea how difficult it is to carry two melting ice cream cones and drive a stick shift?" he asked. She laughed again as she hurried to the kitchen sink. He followed. She turned the water on and grabbed several paper towels and gave them to him then took his cone and placed it in a bowl on the counter. "Thanks."

"You're welcome." She leaned back against the counter and licked her cone as he cleaned and rinsed his hands. "Mmm, this is so good. Thank you. I haven't had French vanilla ice cream in forever, not even in France." She glanced over and saw him watching her lick the cone as he dried his hands. Her insides melted just like the ice cream. He didn't have to utter a word. He just had to look. His eyes said everything. They were the same eyes that haunted her dreams. She tried forgetting him, but it was impossible and now seeing him, she knew why.

He smiled. "I remember how much you love French vanilla."

Looking into his eyes was her undoing. Her stomach shuddered and her heart thudded. At that moment there was nothing else in the room, no one else on the planet, except him. Every nerve in her body seemed to quiver and an onrushing surge of passion swept through her. He was doing this. She quickly looked away and took a deep breath. She needed control. She looked at his cone in the bowl. "You're not finished eating, are you?" she said, her voice noticeably shaken.

He looked at his cone. "Yeah, for now," he said as he continued to watch her eat while drying his hands. "So, when you said before it couldn't be me, what did you mean?" She didn't respond. "Are you seeing anyone seriously these days?" he asked as nonchalantly as possible. She looked at him in warning. "Hey," he raised his hands in surrender, "I'm only asking as a friend. Friends do that, I hear."

"Really, do they?" She smirked sarcastically. He nodded. She assessed his comment then answered, "No, not seriously, not for a while. What about you?"

"After you, impossible."

"I wasn't that bad, was I?" she said jokingly. She closed her eyes, tilted her head and licked her cone halfway around in a slow deliberate action. Always neat and always perfect. He watched, captivated. She opened her eyes to see him observing her every movement. Suddenly everything changed. A surge of sexual heat swirled around them.

"You were right. You are different now," he said, swallowing hard. Their eyes locked.

"Yes, I am," she said, knowing that feeling was getting stronger and stronger. She wanted him and she knew he wanted her. It came automatically as if it had never left. The moment he looked at her, she felt it— the heat, the wanting, the hunger.

"You've slowed down."

"Slowed down? What do you mean?" she asked.

"You were in such a hurry before."

She gazed into his dark eyes. They betrayed nothing of what he really felt. "If I remember correctly, we were both in a hurry."

He smiled. "Yeah, I guess we were," he conceded. "It's funny how things turned out for us."

She licked the cone again, this time not so neat and not so perfect. A small amount smudged her lower lip. She licked, but didn't get it all.

He smiled and nodded. "There's a different kind of edge about you. Definitely not the cut-throat reporter I knew before. Now I see a strong woman with experience and guile, and that's sexy as hell." He paused a moment then continued. "When I said I couldn't stop thinking about you, it was the truth. Do you have any idea how much I want you right now?"

She didn't reply. She couldn't. The echo of her heart pounded against her chest so loudly she barely heard herself think. They stood staring at each other. Yes, she knew he wanted her. She wanted him too. All she had to do was yield to his plea. He took a step toward her and then took the cone from her hand. He placed it onto a dish along with his.

He was masterful at making her want him. He brought everything out in her, the passion, the hunger, the desire and, heaven help her, the need. She didn't just want him. She needed him tonight, now, this very second. This was what she'd been dreaming of for the last three years. One touch was all it took to send her back to where it all began. She licked her lips.

"You missed some right here—may I?" He leaned down and licked her lips and the corner of her mouth.

Her eyes fluttered and her heart raced. She reached up and softly traced the line of his lips with her finger. The passion in his eyes was unmistakable. "Tatiana…" he whispered, then took her hand and licked the creamy, white stickiness from her finger. She watched, spellbound, in breathless awe, anticipating each luscious stroke of his tongue. "You know why I came here, don't you?" he asked, his voice deep and raspy with the swell of passion.

"Tell me," she said seductively.

He turned and dipped his finger into the ice cream. A bit of it slowly slid down the side of his finger and pooled on his fingertip. He held it out as if to let her taste it. But before she opened her mouth, it dripped down onto her chest. The cold white cream slid down her brown skin and slowly trailed the swell of her left breast. Her mouth opened and a tiny gasp escaped.

He leaned in and licked the frozen dessert. The feel of his tongue tasting her, licking her, brought back all kinds of fantasies. The simple act was sensuous beyond belief. His mouth was the perfect weapon and he excelled in his marksmanship. He had used it on her many times before and so very well. Her body trembled just imagining what he'd do next. He slipped her two fingers into his mouth and sucked gently. Then the tip of his tongue nuzzled the tip of her finger. Her arousal level shot through the roof. It was pure eroticism. But she expected nothing less.

"Mmm, I forgot how much I love French vanilla ice cream," he teased. Then, as tenderly and loving as he could, he softly, gently, kissed her lips. The feel of his lips was like the softest whisper. It sent a sweltering surge of heat straight down her spine and between her legs. He kissed her again and again and again.

She shook her head, "Spencer, we shouldn't..." she muttered as he continued. She tried to fight to keep control, but it was useless. Her passion was beyond the tipping point. She surrendered and her sanity flew out the door. "Spencer, we shouldn't be doing this," she whispered then reached up and caressed the side of his face. "You shouldn't be here and I shouldn't be doing this."

"Why not," he asked in a near whisper while kissing her.

"Because I want you too much," she said.

He smiled at her honesty. "Good, I want you too much, too."

"We shouldn't start what we can't finish."

He stopped and looked at her captivating eyes. "Sweetheart, we are finishing this," he assured her.

She leaned slowly and gently toward his lips and kissed him. Then she wrapped her arms around his neck. In an instant he captured her mouth and kissed her with the passion of a dying man. The space between their bodies vanished as he pressed even closer and his tongue delved even deeper. He turned and leaned her back against the counter and pressed his body to hers. His unmistakable arousal sent her need soaring even higher.

Passion erupted as the powerful kiss intensified, harder, stronger, propelling them high, wanting more. He was voracious and she was insatiable. She held tight as he nibbled her neck, her ear and her lips. "I want you. I never stopped. I never will. Seeing you on the beach…"

The rush of arousal was staggering. "Spencer…" she began breathlessly, and then she swallowed her words as he kissed her again, hard and long. Her mind swirled in a lustful haze. She couldn't think anymore. When the kiss finally broke, her lips were swollen with passion.

"You know where this is going," he said simply.

She smiled. "Yes." She knew what was going to happen. She wanted it to happen. She couldn't help herself. How do you resist when every fiber in your being ached for one man's touch? "I don't have any…"

"I do."

He smiled in the way that weakened her knees and made her stomach quiver again. She took his hand and led him through the living room, then upstairs. Her bedroom door was the only one open. As soon as they walked in the kiss came in suddenly with a full force rush of passion. He locked her against the door, barely closing it. Arms wrapped, mouths opened, tongues delving deep, passions bursting. The ravenous hunger of years of separation melted away as their wanton appetite and desire consumed them.

Their sexual hunger had been awakened. Their mouths exploded in delight. There was no beginning or end. There was no him or her. They were one and savoring the mind-blowing kiss was the only thing that mattered. It had been too long since their lips had touched. He pressed into her. She felt the hardness of his erection. It was staggering. He obviously wanted her as much as she wanted him. Then she pushed back. Her heart pounded and her hands shook. They were losing control. Breathless, she looked up at him. His eyes seemed to cut right through her.

They crossed the room to the bed. She turned to him and looked up into his amorous gaze. "Just one night," she promised, but knew she said it more for her than for him.

He nodded his agreement. "Just one night," he repeated. He reached into his pants pocket and pulled out condoms. She took them as he sat down on the side of the bed. She turned around and stepped back. She reached up and untied the thin straps holding the halter in place. The dress loosened and fell to the floor. She stepped out, picked it up and tossed it to the side. She turned around to face him, standing in just her satin bikinis and stiletto sandals. She watched him lick his lips enjoying the sight of her body. "See something you like?"

He didn't speak. He stood up and reached out to her. She blocked his hand, but still moved close. She unbuckled his belt then slowly unbuttoned his shirt. She opened his shirt wide and ran her hands over the smooth surface of his chest. She smiled, remembering how much she loved feeling the deep, hard ridges and the strong, firm muscles of his abs and stomach. His body was magnificent. Touching him was always a secret pleasure she enjoyed.

She pushed the shirt down his arms, letting it drop to the floor at his feet. Then she unzipped his pants. The back of her hand brushed against his erection as they dropped to the floor. She opened the condom packet as he lowered his shorts. He stood naked. She looked down the length of his body, seeing his readiness, and smiled. He stood thick, hard and jutting straight out.

She touched his chest. His body tensed and his stomach jumped. She leaned up and nibbled and kissed his nipple as she touched him again, this time running her fingers lightly down his long, hard thickness. He flinched once more, this time more noticeably. Just thinking about the feel of him inside of her made her juices flow like molten lava. "I remember you liked it when I did this." She leaned closer, letting her already hardened nipples touch his chest, his stomach and the tip of his erection. She stroked him again, this time more ardently. She heard him groan as she repeated the teasing motion.

"You're gonna have to stop doing that."

"You like it, don't you?" she said playfully while continuing her slow, torturous foreplay.

He grabbed her wrists to stop her stroking. "You know I do," he said thickly as he leaned in and kissed her. He stepped back and sat down, bringing her between his legs. He looked down the length of her body. "You were always beautiful, but now you're even more luscious." He removed her panties, then pulled her onto his lap to straddle his legs. He leaned in, captured her lips, then began kissing her chin, her neck and then her breast. When he licked her nipple she pushed back, but he held her securely and captured the other breast and tantalized the nipple with his tongue. Her legs quivered as she watched his slow methodical lips lick and devour her. She held tight to his neck and moaned her pleasure. After a while she leaned back, pressed her hand to his chest and pushed him to lie back on the bed. She climbed on top of him.

Sitting up high, she looked down at him and smiled as she touched him again, running her fingers down his chest, over his abs, to the sweet length of his shaft. He was velvety smooth with tiny veins quivering beneath her touch. He groaned. The primal sound rocked her to the core. With the condom in place at the tip, she eased it down the full length of him. His body twitched as he grabbed her hands. "Woman, you are killing me," he said. His voice was low and husky and barely audible. His eyes darkened and focused intently on her face. This wasn't just sex. This was a reawakening of their latent sexual passion.

She leaned down close to his ear. "That's the whole idea."

He sat up as she still straddled him, pulled her closer then took her breast into his mouth again. She wrapped her arms around his neck as he suckled, tickling the nipple with his tongue. She shivered breathlessly as spikes of ecstasy raged through her. She closed her eyes as her body burned. Then pushed back, but he wouldn't let her go that easily. The more he sucked, licked and teased, the more she wiggled on top of him. It was a vicious circle. Then, unable to take it any longer he rolled her down on the bed and hovered over her.

The quick action took her off guard. She opened her eyes in surprise. He was there smiling down at her. "You feel like screaming for me tonight?" he teased as his hands stroked her.

"So, you think you can make me scream?" she challenged.

He smiled wickedly. "You know I can, so don't tempt me."

She chuckled. "Consider yourself warned," she teased. The laughter stopped as soon as he dipped between her legs. She gasped loudly. Her thighs clenched, but he stayed firm. Her body shook knowing exactly what his intentions were.

His torturous mouth and tongue nibbled and feasted on her body like a condemned man eating his last meal. He was gentle and all consuming. She writhed and shook in uncontrollable torment. "Spencer…" she muttered then licked her lips as her hips began moving in tight precision with his actions. But this wasn't all she wanted from him. "…Come inside," she moaned breathlessly. Either he didn't hear her or he didn't want to stop. The swell of release was coming. Every nerve ending in her body tensed. She was losing control. She needed him to stop now. "Spencer. Enough." He didn't stop. "Spencer. Spencer. I need you, love me now."

He didn't need any more prompting than that. Seconds later he plunged deep into her. She gasped aloud and dug her nails into his back, scratching as the stinging pain engorged her tightness. Her body shook as she held on tight. He retreated then dipped inside again. He was ruthless in his slow, steady torture. In and out, each time he plunged, thrusting deeper and deeper, sending her pleasure beyond limits. Then, in exquisite rapture, she exploded again and again.

She opened her eyes, seeing him looking down at her. His body continued to surge deep inside of her. She felt another wave of passion quickly building. He leaned down and kissed her as she released a scream of pleasure. His body tensed. They came together. Their bodies tightened and strained against the pull of ecstasy.

He collapsed down onto her then rolled to the side positioning her half on top of him. Her body molded to his. Breathless, she laid there feeling the heat of his body connect with hers. She closed her eyes as sleep finally took hold.

Chapter 7

It was midafternoon when Tia finally woke up. She opened her eyes slowly, grimaced and then covered her head with the lightweight cotton sheets. After a while she reached out across the bed feeling the cold cotton beside her. Spencer was long gone. She smiled remembering the night before. Her smile broadened as her body relaxed and stretched out over the comfortable mattress. Closing her eyes again, she touched her lips. The sweet pressure of his kisses was still imprinted on them.

It was the first time in a long time, and having his body pressed to hers was like heaven. He filled her over and over again, and once her pleasure came, he filled her again. She remembered rolling over sometime during the night. She began touching and stroking him. His body reacted to her touch instantly. She found another condom on the floor, climbed on top. And then with slow, deliberate ease, she impaled herself.

Her stomach quivered even now as thoughts of being filled by him started to arouse her once again. Her hips had gyrated up and down and then in and out. She satisfied her need for him with each surge. The rhythmic motion was seductive and sensuous. She had watched as he stared up at her nearly hypnotized by the slow torturous seduction she performed. He held tight, massaging her breasts while tantalizing her nipples. She felt his body tremble and stiffen. She moved faster. A deep husky groan rumbled from his throat as he grabbed her hips and called her name. She climaxed hard and long and drained all she desired from his body. After her release she lay down against him and that was the last thing she remembered.

She smiled. Sex had always been a crucial part of their relationship. Her appetite was equal to his. They enjoyed each other's bodies. It was just that simple. And just like years ago, last night they fulfilled every imaginable desire they had.

She stretched again then sat up and looked around. The room was awash in bright unfiltered sunlight. She got up and walked over to the window and looked out. It was definitely time to get her vacation started and she knew exactly what she was going to do.

She showered and dressed and then went down to

the kitchen to grab leftovers from her takeout meal the night before. When she finished eating, she grabbed a towel and her cell phone and beach bag then headed down to the beach. Seeing two Adirondack chairs, she grabbed one and tossed her bag onto the other.

It was the perfect spot. It was private, but still right there on the beach. She dug in her bag and fished for her eReader. She opened the cover flap and chose her first book. Then she realized she needed to call her sisters. She grabbed her cell and dialed Niki's phone number, but Natalia answered. "Nat? Hey, girl, what's up? I was gonna call you next. I must have gotten the numbers mixed up. I thought I called Niki."

"You did. I'm in the office at the café. Niki's in the kitchen with her hands full. She's doing this huge catering job and she's going nuts with it."

Tia laughed. "I can imagine that. Seriously, I don't know how she does it. She's constantly working."

"Look who's talking," Natalia said.

"All right, don't start. So, tell me, how's married life?"

Natalia giggled. "Actually it's insanely perfect," she said unable to suppress the elation in her voice. "I still can't believe I'm married. It's like we've known each other all our lives. I can't wait until you really get to know him. He's so wonderful."

"It's so romantic and you sound so happy," Tia said.

"I am. I never thought I'd ever feel like this. David is an amazing man and he's so good with the boys. They adore him. They love the idea of seeing their dad on the big screen."

Tia laughed. "Nat, I'm so happy for you. You deserve this."

"Thank you, sweetie. So, listen, Niki told me you're at the cottage. I thought you weren't going this year?"

"Yeah, can you believe it? I changed my mind and the first chance I get to actually take a vacation in three years and I'm all alone here."

"Not for long. As soon as we can, Mia, Niki and I are headed your way. It's going to be great. I can't wait."

"No, you guys don't have to do that. I'm fine here alone."

"Of course we do," Natalia insisted, "we're coming."

"No, Nat, for real. You're still on your honeymoon, for heaven's sake. There's no way I'm taking David's bride away from him just because I'm here by myself."

"Are you kidding, he'd love to spend total guy-time with the boys. Can you imagine all the trouble they'd get into?"

"Well Mia's also newly married and working full-time at the youth center, and I know Niki is crazy busy with the café."

"But, we want to come, really. Everything happened so fast for Mia and me that we never had a real bachelorette party. So it'll be our getaway, too. Just give us a week and we'll be there. Besides, it would be great to see you. It's been forever."

"It hasn't been forever. I was at your wedding just a few months ago."

"That doesn't count," Natalia said. "Wait. Hold on, Niki's coming out of the kitchen. Let me put you on speaker phone. It's Tia," she said to their sister, then put her on loud speaker.

"Hey, did Nat tell you we're coming?"

"Yes, but I was just telling her you guys didn't have to do that. I'm fine."

"We're looking forward to it."

"Actually I was thinking of coming there to you. Martha's Vineyard is a bit crowded these days."

"The island is always crowded this time of year," Nat said.

"That's not the crowded I'm talking about."

"What do you mean?" Niki asked. "Does this have anything to do with your sightseeing yesterday?"

"Sightseeing? Why would you want to go sightseeing?" Nat asked. "You've been going to the Vineyard since you were seven years old. What's left to see?"

"No, not that kind of sightseeing." Niki directed her comment to Nat. "We're talking about the tall, dark and handsome kind of sightseeing. So does it?" Niki asked Tia again.

"Yeah, it was a big mistake. I should have just stayed in or, better yet, left the island."

"Why, what happened?" Nat asked.

"I ran into someone I didn't expect to see."

"Who?" both Niki and Nat asked.

"Spencer Cage," she said. Then there was long silence on the other end of the phone. Tia didn't have to be in the same room to know her sisters were looking at each other with their mouths wide open. "You guys still there?" she finally asked.

"Yeah," they both replied. "Are you okay?" Nat asked.

"I'm fine."

"That's why you got off the phone so quickly yesterday, isn't it? That's when you saw him," Niki said.

"Yeah, I saw him. I was walking on the beach when I was talking to you yesterday. I looked up and there he was just standing there talking on the phone. I couldn't believe it. It's been three years and he was just standing there with his back to me. He wasn't supposed to be here. I was told he was going to be in L.A. doing a video all month."

"Who told you that?"

"His friend, Drill. We've kept in touch over the years. He lets me know where Spencer is whenever I have to come to the States. So I never expected to run into him ever again."

"But you did."

"Yeah, I did."

"So, what happened after he saw you?" Nat asked.

"We talked briefly, awkwardly, and then he invited me to his birthday party at his club here on the island."

"You went didn't you?" Nat asked.

"Of course she didn't," Niki answered assuredly.

"I went. But he wasn't there most of it, so it was fine. It was loud and wild with tons of celebrities and movie stars."

"But you did see him again last night, didn't you?"

"He came by the cottage after I left the party."

"And…?" Both sisters prompted.

"And one thing led to another and we spent the night together." There was the long silence again. This time she didn't say anything either.

"Well, how was it?" Niki asked.

"Niki," Nat chided, "you can't ask her that."

"Sure, I can, how was it?" she asked again.

"Amazing," Tia said. All three giggled like school girls. "He was everything I remember and so much more."

"Where are you now?" Nat asked.

"I'm on the beach."

"Alone?" Niki said.

"Yes. I woke up about an hour and a half ago. He was gone, so I got dressed, ate and came out here. I haven't seen or heard anything from him since."

"Are you okay?" Nat asked.

"Yeah, I'm fine. Look, before you guys get all crazy on me. What happened last night was just a one-time thing, we both agreed. It was physical, that's all. I needed it and he was there. Using his body for sex was perfect for me."

"But Tia…" Nat began.

"Look, Spencer broke my heart once before. I'm not

going to let that happen again. I'm over him. It doesn't mean I can't still want his body."

"We'll be there soon," Niki resolved.

"No, don't come. It's not necessary. To tell you the truth, I'd rather be here alone right now. I need this time for me. With everything going on in my life right now, I'm looking forward to enjoying some quiet time. I'm going to read about five dozen books I've downloaded, sleep all day, eat desserts for breakfast and just relax. So don't worry about me. I'll be fine. And right now you two are interrupting my sleep on the beach time."

"Tatiana…" Niki said.

"I'm fine. Now get off the phone. I'll call you later."

"Okay, talk to you soon."

As soon as Tia hung up she smiled and looked out across the horizon. The water was a soft blue and the sun was blazing bright. It was the perfect day. She relaxed back in her chair and opened her electronic reader again. Halfway through the first chapter of the first book she closed her eyes and fell asleep. She dreamt about floating then swimming and then drowning. Breathless she struggled for air. Heaviness settled in her chest. She felt as if she was now being buried under tons of rocks. She heard screams. She jumped up with a start.

Oh, my God. A frantic memory flash of her running and taking cover shot through her mind instantly. There was chaos. Her heart raced and pounded in her chest as she struggled to get her breath. All she could think was that it was happening again. She looked around frantically. Her dark brown eyes widened as she heard the shrill piercing scream coming from farther down the beach. Panicked, she got up and ran out toward the water. She searched the beach for any signs of trouble. What she found was a playful couple racing toward the water's edge. The woman shrieked with laughter as the man caught up to her, grabbed her waist and caressed her lovingly. She pushed him and ran. He stumbled and chased her down the beach.

Tia released the breath she'd been holding. She looked down at her hands. They were still shaking. She looked around again. There were people walking, swimming and kids playing in the sand. It was just an ordinary day. She took a deep breath and walked back to the shaded chair. She grabbed her towel and beach bag and headed back to the cottage. It was time for a change of scenery.

Spencer stood outside on the terrace close to the beach front. It was midafternoon, so the beach was still relatively crowded. From his vantage point he could see a half mile in either direction. But nothing in particular seemed to keep his interest long. Not even the two young women who constantly paraded by his home in hopes of getting his attention and getting invited inside. They didn't.

"Yo, yo, what up, my man? Where you been?" Riley said as he came out of the house. The two bumped shoulders in greeting.

"What's up?" Spencer said.

"You know, just hanging out. Man, what happened to you last night? I turned around and you were gone. You missed your birthday cake. It was good, too. But don't worry. I ate your piece for you."

Spencer smiled. Riley ate like a vacuum and never gained a pound. Chances are he ate the entire cake. "You all set for the video shoot?"

He looked at his watch. "You know it. It's gonna be hot, too. The place is set up and the techs and extras will be waiting when I get there. In three hours I'm on my way. My bags are already at the hanger," Riley said.

"Good."

"So I gather you're not coming with me," Riley said.

Spencer looked at him. "I still have business to take care of here. Drill's checking out some new tracks for me."

"No worries, I got this," Riley said. "After the video is in the can I've got rehearsals for the promo tour." Just as he said that the two women from earlier on the beach called up to Spencer wishing him a happy birthday. Then they waved to Riley and dropped their tops.

"Yo, damn, man. Did you see that?" Riley exclaimed excitedly. "Yeah, I see why you like coming up here." He laughed happily. "These people are buck wild. They act like they all straight-laced and civilized in the city, and then they come out here and get all freaky." The women waved and flashed once more. "A'ight, that's it, I'm out. I'll check you later. I see the perfect send off."

He slapped and rubbed his hands together then headed to the beach to join the two women.

"Remember, you got three hours," Spencer said.

"No problem," Riley said. The two women waved and motioned for him to join them, too. He just nodded his head and watched as they walked down the beach. Spencer turned and headed back inside. Ultimately he was restless. Tired of being inside, and now tired of being outside. He tried to get work done earlier, but found his focus wasn't there. As soon as he opened the sliding door and stepped inside the house, a rush of chilly air hit him. Drill was still here. No one else insisted on blasting the air conditioner like he did. Spencer went to the kitchen and grabbed a bottle of water. He opened it and walked back to the living room to stand at the large windows.

For some reason the house seemed particularly empty today, or maybe it was just him feeling empty. Getting up and leaving Tia's bed this morning was hard. But he did it. He had to. He knew he was going to have to do a lot of things he didn't want to do, including pretending to fall in love with her. She had to believe what he wanted her to believe. Right now he needed her to believe everything was good between them with the possibility of more.

Thinking about Tia instantly brought a single memory from their time together. Barely noticeable, a sly smile tipped the corner of his mouth. He allowed himself that souvenir. When he woke up the covers were tangled at the foot of the bed and she was lying on her stomach. The easy sway of her bare shoulders and back gave way to the most delicious rear he'd ever seem. Two perfectly rounded cheeks. He ran his hand along her gentle curves. Her delicate brown skin seemed to burn his fingers and ignite his body. Waking up he was already hard and just looking at her naked body made his blood pool in one area. All he wanted to do was touch her again. She'd wake up and he'd bury himself between her legs.

It would have been fair play, his turn. Sometime during the early morning he awoke feeling her touching him. It was a welcome surprise. Then she climbed on top of him and impaled herself. She was bold and aggressive in her desires. Gone was the demure lover he once knew. She was the same, but different. He liked the new her. Either way, she still made his body burn. All he kept thinking about was waking her up and making love to her again. But he didn't. He did, however, touch her once more before he left.

He smiled as he thought about her sleeping body. The muscles in his neck tensed. But he knew he had to control his emotions. This wasn't about him, this was about his company. He opened the studio door and walked in. Drill was there listening to the two new tracks he'd laid down yesterday. It was his job to clean them up and add the polish. He'd been in there for the last two hours. Spencer wasn't worried that he wouldn't like the songs. He knew he would. He sat down at the board and plugged in his earphone. "My Itch" was playing. He nodded his head to the heavy, gyrating beat. The base line was deeper and the treble intensified. It sounded really good. Drill had added the perfect touches to take it to the next level.

As the song was ending, he removed his headphones and waited for Drill to do what he needed to do. Drill leveled the equalizer to fade out then lowered his headphone around his thick neck. He nodded his head approvingly. "Man, that shit is on the money. You got that."

"You like it," he confirmed.

"Hell, yeah," Drill said. His smile was endless. He leaned back in the chair and pressed the play button again. "Under the Top," played. They listened in silence, both nodded to the slow, sultry beat. The song was more soulful and moodier, with a rich melody and lyrics that touched every emotion. Drill had done a great job finishing it. "Yo, check this, I like this part right here." They listened closely. "Hear that, that's it. That's the one right there. Yeah, see that's tight, right there." He reached out with his fist. Spencer pounded it. "You got that. You didn't need me to do anything to them. The lyrics are on the money. See, I knew seeing Tia was a good thing. She got you writing again."

Spencer smiled and nodded. He knew the two new songs were tight, but hearing Drill's positive affirmation made it even better. He also knew Drill was right; Tia was his motivation.

"A couple more of these and you got your CD. I figure, what, you see your girl tonight and by tomorrow you're done." He chuckled.

Spencer smiled. "I don't know about all that."

"Man, you know she's the one that gets you going. Can't nobody write like you when she's around. I swear if there is such a thing as a Muse, she'd be yours."

"Let me hear 'My Itch' again."

Drill pressed a few buttons on the massive board in front of them then held his earphones to one hear. He listed a few seconds and then pointed when the song was coming up. Spencer put his earphones back on and listened. This track was faster with a reckless beat that almost rocked the room. It was loud and brash and full of energy. Spencer smiled. He had tweaked it after he came home this morning. What was once a song about lust was now a hot song about sexual conquest.

When the track went off, Drill turned to him shaking his head. "I don't know what you were thinking when you wrote this one. But, damn, man, you hit this one out of the park. The clubs are gonna be jumping when this hits. I've already got some ideas for the remix track. I'm gonna need the full board for that, so I'm headed to Atlanta later. I can see a trifecta and more on this one. Tops on the pop, R&B, hip-hop, dance and rock charts."

"We'll see," Spencer said, standing. "I'm headed into town. You want anything?"

"Yeah, I need some coffee," Drill said, then turned back to the board, "and not that fake stuff. Get me something dark and roasted. Real coffee, so I can taste it."

"Yeah, all right," Spencer said.

"Hey," Drill added, "you know it was good seeing Tia again last night. She looks fantastic."

Spencer stopped at the studio door. "Yes, she does."

"You know the two of you were always good together," Drill added, then motioned to the board. "Hell, you saw her less than twenty-four hours ago and you got two hit tracks here. You need to be careful with this game you're playing. You just might get played yourself in the end. Love always gets its way."

"I'll see you later," Spencer said, then walked out.

Drill shook his head. He knew trouble coming when he saw it. Spencer was headed for trouble. He just didn't know it yet.

Chapter 8

Before leaving the cottage, Tia made a list of everything she needed to take care of while she was in town. Her first stop, to the car rental, was essential. She needed transportation for the rest of the month. She rented a MINI Cooper two-door convertible. It was small and cute and exactly what she needed to get around the island. As soon as she got in and pulled off, she drove right into oncoming traffic. Horns blew and people screamed, reminding her that she was driving on the wrong side of the road. She hadn't realized how living in London for the last three years had affected her driving. Afterward she made a concerted effect to drive on the right side of the road.

With that behind her, the plan was simple. Drive

into town and purchase the basics, and then head to the farmer's market and fish market for fresh fruit, vegetables and seafood. She drove to the local grocery store first. Her sister Niki, an accomplished chef, usually did the shopping and cooking when they stayed on the island, but since she was on her own for a while she decided to try her cooking skills. It had been a long time since she shopped and cooked for herself. With her busy work schedule, she seldom had time to cook and rarely shopped for more than one or two days at a time.

She parked the car, grabbed a shopping cart then went inside. The cottage kitchen was amply supplied with cooking utensils and basic seasonings, but she needed a few more ingredients like turmeric, cardamom, white peppercorns and couscous. When she cooked, she usually prepared meals from her travels. She collected recipes from all over the world. Moroccan food was her favorite and her cooking specialty.

Unable to find what she needed at the first store, she tried two more. She found the balance of what she needed at the third, a small international market on the outskirts of town. While standing in line at the checkout counter, she noticed the cover of a magazine she used to work for. It was her first job out of college and the job that started everything for her. She picked it up and flipped through.

It was the exact same format written by the exact same people about the exact same celebrities. Nothing much had changed. She couldn't believe she actually worked there for as long as she did. Editorially, the magazine was pure celebrity drivel. It was a hairbreadth from tabloid reporting. It wasn't until she'd written her first article and had it edited with a sensationalized angle that she realized the line between real journalism and what she did was massive.

She flipped to and read the table of contents and was surprised to find something on Mason Brooks. She turned to the page. The article talked about Mason's life, his contribution to the music industry and his sudden death. But it was nothing she didn't already know. There were several photographs of him and one candid shot of him and Spencer together. In it Spencer was sitting at a desk and looked extremely pensive. She smiled, wondering what he was thinking about at that moment. He stared directly into the camera. His eyes were intense yet lost and seemed so far away. It was as if he was staring right at her.

The line moved. Tia stepped forward still wondering about the photo of Spencer. She still couldn't believe he was here on the island. And the fact that they'd made love the night before was totally unreal. Her stomach quivered just thinking about it. He was just as she remembered, but better. Their lovemaking was fast and ferocious the first time. It was sultry, heated and passionate. Later when she climbed on top of him, they'd taken their time. It was slow and erotic. She closed her eyes and took a deep breath. She could almost feel his hand on her hips, his mouth on her breasts, the taste of his lips and the smell of his cologne, the sound of his…

"Interesting reading."

Tia was startled, then went still. She knew that voice. There was no mistaking the deep masculine timbre that always cut right through her. She looked up and then turned around slowly seeing Spencer standing in the line behind her. She had no idea how long he'd been standing there watching her flip through the pages of the magazine. He smiled seductively as he stepped closer to her. "Hi," he said smiling broadly.

"Hi," she breathed. "What are you doing here?" she asked.

"Shopping," he said innocently, holding up his basket with only one item inside.

She peeked in. "Coffee? Since when do you drink coffee?"

"I don't, Drill does. How are you feeling?" he asked.

"Fine, rested, and you?" she asked, trying to sound as nonchalant as possible. The last thing she wanted was to draw attention to them standing there. But the mere fact that Spencer Cage was there drew stares, smiles and opened gestures of recognition and acknowledgements.

"Never better. I slept very well," he said. His smile spread wider. "How's the jetlag?"

"Over. Thank you for asking."

"Pity, I kinda liked you with jetlag. You were adventurous," he said softly for her ears only.

Tia looked around seeing several women watching them and smiling. Even though their conversation sounded meaningless on the surface, anyone could look in her face and see there was something between them. Ordinarily it wouldn't bother her, but for some reason now it did.

"I didn't expect to see you."

"I know. I didn't expect to see you, either. Since when do you go to grocery stores?"

"I do a lot of things I didn't do before."

"Yes, you do," she affirmed, knowing exactly what he was talking about. She was next in line to check out. "Why don't you go ahead of me? I have a lot more and you only have one thing. I'll take longer."

"I wouldn't think of it. I insist, after you."

She nodded and began putting her items on the counter. The cashier was so busy looking at Spencer that she rang up two of Tia's items incorrectly. With that straightened out, Tia paid her bill and then turned to Spencer. "It was good seeing you again. Have a good day." She grabbed her two grocery bags then hurried out. He followed a few minutes later meeting her halfway to her car.

"Need some help?" he said, then slipped the bags from her hand before she could respond. He followed her to the car and placed the bags in the trunk with the other groceries.

Tia walked to the driver's side as Spencer approached just in time to open the door for her. "Thank you."

"We still need to talk about that proposition I have for you, how about dinner this evening around eight o'clock?"

"Actually I'm cooking dinner myself tonight. But you can tell me what you have in mind now."

He chuckled. "Wait, wait, you're cooking? Since when do you cook? I thought your sister Niki was the cook in the family."

"She is, but I cook, as well."

He nodded approvingly. "That's good to know. So, what are you cooking tonight?"

"It doesn't really have a name. It's kind of Moroccan inspired from a dish I had in Tangier a few years ago. The closest would be a tagine seafood dish with vegetables, couscous, fruit and nuts. But since I don't have a tagine, I'm going to improvise and use a hibachi."

"Mmm, sounds tasty."

"It is, very tasty."

"What's a tagine?"

"It's an earthen cooking pot with a conical shaped lid. It's used in a lot of Moroccan and North African cuisine."

"Do you have one at home?"

"Yes, but it's not the kind of thing you just lug around from place to place." She got into the car and inserted the key in the ignition. Just then her cell phone rang. She grabbed it and looked at caller ID. "Portman," she muttered, then answered and listened a few seconds and replied she wasn't interested.

Spencer tensed. He knew who Portman was—Donavan's attorney. Apparently he was trying to make his move. "Where to now?" he asked when she ended the call.

"I have more shopping to do."

"Why don't I stop by the house later and we can talk."

"Okay, that'll be great. I'll talk to you later."

She started the car, waved and drove off. At the first traffic light down the street she stopped and looked up in the rearview mirror. Spencer was still standing where she left him. She shook her head then glanced at her reflection. "Girl, what are you doing with him?" When the light changed she put on her sunglasses and continued her day.

Twenty minutes later Tia was across the island in Chilmark at the local shopping area and seafood and vegetable market. She stopped in a few stores and window shopped before heading to the vegetable and seafood market. As she walked along the wharf she paused to lean against the rail and watch the boats come and go. There were dozens all lined up, some huge and elaborate and others simple sailing vessels. It had been a long time since she been out on the water. She made a mental note to take a sailing trip around the island.

She started thinking about her future. Staying at her present job wasn't going to happen. It wasn't that she was miserable where she was or with what she did, she wasn't. She was just tired of the drama and pain she constantly saw. She needed a change. Coming back to the States was the first thing she needed to do. She missed her family and friends. And now that her sister was married, she realized somewhere down the line she wanted to have a family of her own.

"Hello, again." Tia turned around quickly seeing Spencer leaned on the rail beside her. "I hated disturbing you. You looked lost in thought."

"Spencer, what are you doing here?" she asked.

He didn't turn to look at her, but kept his eyes forward looking out at the view. "I know you're gonna think I'm following you, but I swear I'm not. I'm here to get my boat ready for tomorrow."

She looked at him skeptically. "Your boat. Right."

"It's the truth."

"So of all the boat docks on the island your boat is moored at this one."

"Coincidence," he offered.

"That would be a mighty big coincidence." She turned and looked across the water at the dozens of boats moored at the dock. "So, which one's your boat?" she asked shielding her eyes from the bright sun.

He pointed across the water to one of the boat slips nearest the outlet. "That one, second one from the end," he said pointing to a large vessel with a dark blue, gold and purple stripe on the side. "I just finished rigging it for tomorrow." She followed his line of vision, seeing a big sleek vessel with double sails tied down.

"That's yours? Wow, it's beautiful. It looks like it's

fast on the water." She nodded with interest. "What kind is it, a cruiser or a racer?"

He smiled looking at her impressed. "Whoa, it sounds like the lady knows a little something about boats."

"No, not at all, I can never figure out the whole port, starboard, bow and the stern thing. I can, however, tie a pretty nifty square knot."

He chuckled. "Okay, that's good to know. It's simple. The bow is the forward part of a boat, the stern is the back part, the port is the left side and the starboard is the right side when facing forward. And to answer your first question, it's a Beneteau First Series. It's the new racing series."

"Do you know how to sail it?"

"Yes, of course," he said.

"Really?" she said, sounding more than a little skeptical.

"For real," he insisted.

"So it's for racing, right? Don't tell me you're racing sailboats now?"

"Not yet, but I hope to soon."

"Really," she said, looking at him in awe. "Since when do you have an interest in sailing or racing?"

"Since I was a kid," he said, then looked down at the water lapping against the pier. "My dad used to take me to the Conservatory Waters in Central Park. It was right on the east side off Fifth Avenue. It's one of the few good things I remember about him. They had weekend miniature sailboat races. We'd spend the whole day watching those small boats on the pond. We couldn't afford one of course, at least nothing like what we saw. But we still loved watching them. Those were perfect days for me. Going out on the water now reminds me of that time."

She nodded. There was a sense of loss in his voice. Spencer never talked about his father, so she was surprised he not only mentioned his father but had such a fond memory of him. She wanted to ask more about their relationship, but she didn't want the moment to come off like an interview. They were just getting to know each other again and she didn't want to jeopardize this new beginning. "You never talk about your family."

"No, I don't," he said evenly, then looked back at her. "I have an idea. I'm headed to Nantucket tomorrow for a long weekend. Why don't you come with me?"

"Nah, that's okay. You and your boys enjoy."

"Riley left for L.A this afternoon and Drill is leaving for Atlanta this evening. I'm all alone."

The way he said he word 'alone' made her question his meaning. He seemed to imply more emphasis than he consciously intended. Although maybe she was reading too much into his words, but it sounded as if he was actually—lonely. "What's in Nantucket?"

"They have a restaurant I like to go to whenever I'm in the Vineyard and get a chance."

"You're gonna take your boat all the way to Nantucket just to have some seafood."

"Sure, why not?" he said, and then continued, "Plus I'm also checking out a business opportunity and meeting up with some people Saturday evening. And of course, it's an opportunity to be out on the water. Sailing to Nantucket is the perfect weekend trip. It's not too long or too short and the waters are usually calm and it affords me the chance to relax and cruise there. It's a nice, easy run, so why don't you join me? It'll be fun."

"Thanks, but I think I'd better pass."

"May I ask why?"

"Spencer, where do you think this is going between us?"

"What do you mean?"

"I mean after last night. We made love. What happened was great, it was more than great, but I don't think it would be a good idea to keep seeing each other like this."

"Why not?"

"Last night was probably a huge mistake and, to tell you the truth, I'm conflicted about this. We cut ties for three years and now all of the sudden we're hanging out together. I don't want to get hurt again and I don't want to hurt you."

"Tia, it's just a boat ride across the sound. No big deal. It's not like I'm proposing marriage. Nantucket is a beautiful island. They have great restaurants, great shopping and the trip over there is peaceful and relaxing. I thought since you were on vacation you might want to take a short trip."

Suddenly she felt silly. He was right, it *was* no big deal. They would be just two friends hanging out. It was simple. She nodded. Maybe she *was* reading too much into what happened between them. "Okay, I'll think about it."

"Sounds good, but while you're thinking about it, pack for a few days and nights, and don't forget your boat shoes. The deck can get slippery."

"I don't have boat shoes," she said.

"I guess I'm gonna have to do something about that."

"No, please don't. There's not a lot of reasons to wear boat shoes in London or other places I travel to. If I go, I'll wear my running shoes."

He looked around the waterfront. "So what exactly are you doing here?" he asked changing the subject.

"I was just about to head down to the market and pick up some fresh seafood for dinner. Then I stopped and looked around seeing how much the island has changed over the years. It's really amazing." She paused a moment then turned to him. "You know you never did tell me about this proposition you have for me. What is it exactly?" she asked.

"Are you hungry? I assume you don't eat breakfast still, so how about a late lunch."

"Sure, okay. Where to?"

"Come on, I know the perfect place."

She nodded. They began walking along the pier,

talking about the changes she remembered over the years. They passed the seafood and vegetable markets and continued to the end of the pier. They finally stopped at a dilapidated-looking restaurant called The Ramshackle. It was popular for its deceptive decor. The outside was an eyesore, but the inside was stunning. She stood smiling. "Oh, wait, I know this place. Mr. Cartwright owns it."

"Yeah, that's right."

"I haven't been here in years. I forgot all about it. My parents used to bring us here sometimes. That was long before all the newer restaurants came to town. The first time I saw it I was like, eww, no way, then we went inside and I loved it. I remember they have the best clam chowder on the planet."

"Come on, let's get a seat outside."

She nodded, but silently a red flag immediately went up. The idea of sitting outside in a café-styled setting sent shivers through her. She knew it was something she was just going to have to work through, but not today. "Actually, do you mind if we sit inside to eat?"

"No, either way works for me."

They went into the restaurant. The hostess directed them to the outside seating since the inside tables were all occupied and there was far more privacy outside. She conceded and they were directed to a waiting table. As soon as Spencer passed through the dining area, there was a constant buzz in the room. Heads turned and people stopped eating and stared. She barely noticed. As she sat down, she looked around nervously. Intellectually she realized that this wasn't Istanbul and the likelihood of a terrorist attack was remote at best, still she remained tense and on edge.

As soon as their drink orders were given, Spencer noticed a change in Tia. She was tense, nervous and closed off. She looked around uneasily. "Are you okay?" he asked.

"Yes, fine," she said tightly.

"We can go somewhere else if you'd like."

"No, this is fine," she said, smiling weakly.

He watched as she took a deep breath and tried to focus on him. But he saw the struggle in her eyes. She smiled, but it was obvious it never reached her heart. He reached across the table and took her hand. "Tia, tell me about your travels."

"Wow, that's a hard one. That could take forever. I've gone so many places and done so many things. And each place I've learned so much about the people and their cultures."

"What was your favorite location?"

"All of them," she joked with ease, seeming more relaxed.

He chuckled. "Okay, how about where you go on vacation."

"Actually this is my first vacation in three years."

"So you've been working nonstop."

"Something like that. But if I had to choose a location I'd say it was Africa, all of it, from Morocco to

Mozambique. And if I had to choose just one place it would have to be Madagascar. The beaches are breathtaking. The sand is so fine it squeaks when you walk on it. My ultimate fantasy is to swim naked in the channel and live on the beach for a year, no cell phones, no work and no drama."

"Now that sounds fascinating."

She smiled shyly and blushed. "I can't believe I just told you that."

"Why? I think it's great. Do you mind if I share your fantasy?"

"No, not at all," she said.

Their drinks were served and they placed their meal order. They talked easily about her time on Martha's Vineyard as a child and her hometown of Key West. She was surprised to learn that he'd never been there. She gave him a standing invitation to visit anytime. After the meal was served and eaten they sat enjoying their renewed friendship. "So you mentioned you were interested in finding a new opportunity," he said.

"Global International News is serious journalistic work. It's national, international, business, politics, health, entertainment, sports and travel news reported twenty-four hours a day. It's what I thought I wanted— to be taken seriously as a journalist. After the fluff celebrity stuff I used to do with the magazine, I welcomed the opportunity to expand and learn. And in all fairness, I got to travel and experience so many different and incredible things. I met people from all around the world and it was exciting. Sure there was sometimes danger…"

"Like in Istanbul," he speculated.

She nodded. "And in other places, as well. I reported form the Middle East, Pakistan, China, South America. Wherever they sent me, I found and reported a story. It was my dream job."

"So what happened?" he asked.

She looked away. "I guess I just don't feel it anymore."

"What do you mean? Feel what?"

"I mean I don't feel the empathy anymore. I'm starting not to care and that doesn't feel right to me. It's like I turned my emotions off like a light switch. People were suffering and dying all round me and all I could do was to get the story and report it."

"It was your job. Isn't that how you have to be to report the kinds of things you report, stay focused and detached?"

"For some it works, but no, not me. Whenever I do a story I need to have a connection to my stories and the people I'm talking about and introducing to the rest of the world. If I don't have feelings and care about them, how is someone else going to?"

"So what's next for you?"

"I don't know yet. I actually thought about launching my own news website."

"Wow, that sounds like a great idea. You'd be really good."

"It's a thought, nothing serious yet. I have time."

"Good," he said.

She looked at him like he was unfeeling. "Why good?"

"Because, like I mentioned before, I have a proposition for you," he said.

"Okay, what is it?"

"I need a writer."

"Okay, I can give you a few names of some really good writers I know. Also, my agent handles quite a few…"

"No," he interrupted, "I need you to do it."

"You need me to do what exactly?"

"Interview me and write an article."

"What kind of article?" she asked curiously.

"There are going to be some major changes at the company. I need you to do what you did for Mason and BoomBox. I need you to reintroduce me to the world."

"Reintroduce you," she repeated. "Are you kidding? Who on the planet doesn't already know who you are?"

"They know the name and the facade, not me. It's time."

She knew what he was saying, but she wasn't sure if he knew all it entailed. She stared at him a moment before answering. She could see he was very serious. Spencer, with all his fame and notoriety, was a public sensation, but a private wonder. He was right, no one really knew much about him or his past, including her. "As tempting as it sounds, I can't."

"Why not?" he asked.

"First of all, I'm under exclusive contract with Global. It would be a legal conflict to write for another company while employed there," she said. He nodded, seeming to consider his options. "But I don't understand. If a magazine or some media outlet wants to interview you, there'll be a writer assigned to do the job. You don't have to hire your own freelancer."

"What if I offer Global the interview as an exclusive? The only stipulation being you interview me, no one else."

Her heart jumped. An interview like this could put her career back on the fast-track. "I'm not in the entertainment division. I'm in the world news division."

"Anything's possible," he said with conviction. "This could be your last interview before starting your news website or it could be the start of the site."

"I'd have to think about it."

He smiled and nodded. He knew right then that he had her. It was only a matter of time before she said yes.

Chapter 9

Spencer maneuvered through the heavy afternoon traffic with ease as he headed back to his house. He caught a quick glimpse of himself in his rearview mirror, and then quickly looked away. He wasn't proud of what he did, but he knew it had to be done. It was the first step, so there was no need to feel pleased. He told her what he needed her to believe and she believed it. So for that he didn't smile or congratulate himself. What he was doing wasn't his style and certainly wasn't in his nature. He didn't like playing games and manipulating people. That was his father's expertise. And he was nothing like his father. But right now he didn't have a choice. He wasn't going to let this rest. He needed to know answers and, one way or another, she was going to give them to him.

He smirked, knowing that the one man who would have been proud of his actions today would never know what he did. The bitter taste of bile rose up in his mouth. It always happened when he thought about his father, his real father, and remembered the few good times they spent together. He thought about the story he told Tia. It was the truth, he and his father did spend time at the pond in Central Park, but what he didn't mention was that the man who took him to the pond wasn't actually his father. It was his great-uncle Elwood. It was the first of many fabrications he intended to tell her for the article.

She didn't accept yet, but he knew she would. There was no way she'd turn an opportunity like this down. She was a reporter in her heart and a no-bars-held interview with him was too tempting to resist. All he had to do now was keep the pretense up. And he knew the perfect people to help, even if they wouldn't know they would be. He pushed the phone button on the steering wheel. There was a dial tone through the car sound system. He said the name and waited for the call to connect. The receiver was picked up on the third ring. "Hi, Mom, it's Spencer."

"Hi, son. Now, I hope you still coming by tomorrow? Because I don't want to hear any foolishness about you not coming to see us because you're too busy working," she warned. "I know you have all these companies that need your attention, but you need to take a few minutes to stop and visit your family, too. Love feeds your soul—remember that."

"There's no way I'd call to cancel. I can't wait. I'm taking the boat over just in case you want to go for a ride around the island again."

She laughed. "Now what in the world would I look like getting on that thing again," she said between bouts of laughter. "You got me there once—shame on me if I set foot on that thing again. I prayed and I gave the good Lord my solemn word last time that I would never step foot on that thing again if he got me off in one piece. So, no, thank you, that boat of yours is too fast for me."

Spencer laughed. Claire Jackson was actually his great-aunt, his grandmother's sister. He had always called his aunt and uncle Mom and Dad. He called his real parents by their first names. Claire was married to Elwood, his great-uncle. They worked and lived in Boston all their lives. They didn't have any children, so when he was young, he was sent out of the city to stay with them every summer.

Then when they retired and he made it big in the industry, he asked them where in the world they wanted to live. They chose Nantucket. A few months later he bought them a huge mansion on the island. His aunt Claire hated it. They finally accepted a nice-sized beach house with a white picket fence and a walkway lined with pink, purple and blue hydrangea bushes. It was quaint and elegant and perfect for them.

"Mom, I just called to let you know I might be bringing someone with me, a friend."

"A female friend?" Claire asked.

"Yes," Spencer said.

"Not one of those fly-by-night, money hungry, skinny little things I see hanging all on you at those awards shows."

"No," Spencer said, chuckling at his aunt's unabashed opinion, "she's nothing like them. You're going to like her." He said the words and knew she would. Tia was the kind of woman his aunt always wanted for him. She was kind and intelligent and strong. She was also going to hate him after everything was over.

"Are you serious about her?" she asked.

He didn't respond right away. "We've known each other a long time."

"I'm not senile, son, that wasn't the question I asked. I asked you if you're serious about her."

Knowing there was no way she was going to let him dodge the question a second time, he answered. "I was at one time, but now…"

"You're not sure," she said, finishing for him.

"There are things between us," he added.

"Is she married, engaged or seeing someone else?"

"No, none of those," he said.

"Then what could possibly be between you?"

"Things," he repeated evasively.

"Spencer, son, you're thirty-two years old. Don't you think it's about time you get yourself sure? Now I'm not pressing you, but we're not getting any younger on this end. It's about time you think about settling down and having babies. I want to spoil some great-grandnieces and nephews while I still can."

"Mom, she and I have a history that's not easily erased."

"Any and everything can be erased if you love her."

He heard conversation in the background. It was his uncle Elwood. An instant later another receiver picked up. "Claire, would you please let the man live his life and have some fun. He works all the time. He's still young, and he's got all these women after him. There's not a thing wrong with that. You go on, son, and have some fun before you settle down. Don't worry, when the right woman comes along, you'll know it. Won't be nothing in the world that's gonna keep you apart."

"Thanks, Dad. All right, so I'll see you guys tomorrow. Do you need me to bring anything?" he asked.

"Just bring yourself and your friend. See you tomorrow."

Spencer pressed the button on the steering wheel, disconnecting the call. Calling his mom and dad was like calling his conscience. Claire's words echoed in his mind, *Any and everything can be erased if you love her.*

He knew he still had feelings for Tia. A part of him knew he'd always have feeling for her. No matter how far apart they were, she was still with him. No other woman had ever made him feel so complete. But he couldn't think about that right now. He had to get through this and move on. He needed to stay focused on his end goal to save his company by any means necessary.

He pressed another button on the steering wheel and the car radio turned on. The DJ was playing a track from one of his most recently signed artists. It was a song he'd written and had personally produced, then had Drill edit the remix. It was released a week ago and was already number two on four major charts. He nodded his head to the beat. It sounded good. For the first time in a long time he felt accomplished. Everything was going as he planned. And without knowing it, his aunt and uncle would do exactly what he expected, be his family.

Now all he had to do was make sure Tia went with him to Nantucket. He pulled into his driveway, parked and got out. He went inside and looked around as he headed to the bar. Being alone didn't bother him, he preferred it, but tonight he had no intention of being alone. He poured himself a drink and downed it in one gulp. He poured a second drink and carried it to the living room and collapsed on the sofa. He flipped through the cell phone messages he missed all afternoon. Nothing was majorly important. He took a deep breath and stared out through the massive floor-to-ceiling windows overlooking the back terrace. He stood and walked over to the window. The world was his. He had everything any man could possible want. Then he stopped right there. He knew what was supposed to come next.

His aunt's words came to him again. *Any and everything can be erased if you love her.* "Love isn't always enough," he said aloud, then turned and headed to the recording studio. He worked for the next four hours. Afterward he went upstairs to take shower and change clothes. Tia was about to have an unexpected dinner guest.

Tia was shocked by Spencer's proposition. She drove back to the cottage in a perpetual state of gleeful apprehension. She couldn't stop thinking about their conversation and his proposition. She was speechless at the time and didn't give him a yes or no answer. Her gut was telling her to pass, but her head was telling her, since the timing was so perfect, to jump on it. Still, she was no fool. She knew there had to be more to it.

Spencer wanted something. She just didn't know what it was. There's no way he'd go from furious with her to giving her the interview of her career in so short a time. He hadn't done an interview since Mason's book was released years ago. Then when Mason died months ago, he went into total reclusive mode. There was something more going on. By all accounts she'd be insane to even consider doing it without knowing everything, but then again, she'd be insane to pass up the opportunity to find out what.

She was flattered, of course. Who wouldn't be? Spencer Cage was huge. Everyone knew him as a brilliant media mogul who spun gold as a music producer and entrepreneur. His reputation in the industry was unparalleled. His name, his image, his companies were worldwide. But his past and personal life was always off limits. No one knew much about his early life, not even his friends. Doing an in-depth interview on him would get her right back where she was. And the fact that he hadn't done an interview since Mason died would only increase its significance. She knew her network had been trying to get him for years. So for her to so easily get him would be major. They'd have to take notice.

When she got to the cottage, she put her groceries away then grabbed a glass of wine and stepped outside onto the porch. The peaceful serenity of the moment stilled her. She thought about what Spencer has asked of her. She had no idea what she was going to do. She called her sisters, but neither picked up. A few minutes later her cell phone rang. She expected it to be one of her sisters, but it was her cousin's wife, Mia. "Hi, Mia, what's up?"

"Nothing, I just thought I'd call to keep you company for a while. I heard you're in Martha's Vineyard vacationing. I was just there two years ago with my half sisters, Janelle and Nya."

"How are they? I haven't seen them since your wedding."

"They're fine. As a matter of fact I just spoke with them. So, how's the weather there? It's raining and miserable here."

Tia looked around, smiling at the brightness of the late afternoon. "The sun is out, the sky is a mellow blue and the breeze is just warm enough to be pleasant."

Mia laughed. "Okay, now you're just rubbing it in."

"No, really," Tia said as she continued looking around. "I'm standing out on the back porch and the view of the Atlantic is spectacular. I can't believe I canceled last year and went to Tibet instead. Do you know what the weather is like in Tibet this time of year? There was rain and landslides almost daily. Being here now is just like heaven."

"I hope you haven't been hanging around the house all day? Girl, you need to get out and have some fun. Janelle was there two months ago. She told me there's a great new club on the island. Why don't you go there tonight? I have no idea what kind of club it is, but she said it was awesome. She had a blast. She's talking about heading up to The Vineyard in September."

"It is nice. It's called The Cage. It's huge and the DJ plays all kind of music, rap, hip-hop, island reggae and calypso."

"Sounds like you've already been there?" Mia asked.

"I have, last night."

"Did you have a good time?"

"Yes, it was nice, but I was so exhausted and jet-lagged. I left early and came home."

"Jet-lagged? Why on earth did you go out last night?"

"I was invited. Spencer Cage owns it."

"Spencer Cage as in the Spencer Cage, the music producer?" she said.

"Yes."

"Now that's a name I haven't heard in years. He seemed to just drop off the radar a while back. I wonder what he's up to now."

"Actually, he's fine. He's here. He invited me to the club."

"Wait, what do you mean, he's here, he invited you? Do you know him personally?"

"Yes, we were together a few years back. We ran into each other on the beach when I first got here. He invited me to the club to celebrate his birthday."

"Whoa, wait a minute. That's right, you wrote the book on Mason Brooks. That's how you know him."

"That's also when we broke up. He wasn't too pleased about the book. Apparently there was way too much truth in it."

"He's not still upset about it, is he?"

"We talked. We're trying to go beyond all that."

"Good, I'm glad to hear that," Mia said. "So what was it like seeing him again after so many years?"

"At first it was tense and uncomfortable, but then we just started talking like we used to. He invited me to his birthday party. I went," Tia said.

"Are you going to see him again?"

"I don't know. I was just wondering that same thing, too."

"You said you were together, you mean the two of you had a relationship?"

"Yes."

"Do you still have feelings for him?"

"Yes, I do. I guess I always have and probably always will," Tia said.

"It sounds like a romance in the making."

"I don't know about a romance in the making. We just have a good time together. A lot of it's physical, we enjoy each other."

"Nothing wrong with that—enjoy."

"So what's going on with you?" Tia asked, changing the subject.

"Actually, I called to give you some good news."

Tia started smiling. She got excited even before Mia said the words. Everyone in the family had been expecting this news. "Tell me, tell me, tell me."

"I'm pregnant."

Tia screamed, then quieted down and looked around. She screamed again, this time not as loud. The joy in her heart was overflowing. "Oh, Mia, I'm so happy for you and Stephen. You both are going to be incredible parents. How are you, how's the baby?"

"I'm fine and the baby's growing beautifully."

"How's Stephen?" Tia asked of her cousin.

"He's fantastic, walking on cloud number nine."

"Oh, I'm so happy for you. So, wait, how far along are you?"

"I'm four months."

"Four months, already," Tia exclaimed.

"We'd been trying for a while and then I caught a cold and was sick for almost three weeks. I was pregnant and didn't even know it."

"Oh, Mia, I'm so happy for you and Stephen."

"Listen, I hate to share good news and then run, but I'm at the center and I hear a ruckus starting up in the hall. I have to go and see what's going on."

"Go, I'll catch up with you later. Take care and congratulations. I wish you and Stephen all the best. Give him a big hug for me." Tia hung up beaming. She was overjoyed for her cousin and his wife. New life in the family always brought everyone together. She was definitely going to head down to Key West before going back to London.

She turned to go back inside just as her cell phone rang again. It was her sister Natalia. She answered. "Hey, it's me. Hold on, Niki wants to conference in." She got off the line for a moment then returned. "Hey, I'm here."

"Me, too," Niki said. "What's going on?"

Tia was still grinning. "Did you hear the good news?"

"About Mia and Stephen? I know isn't it wonderful," Nat said.

"I know, isn't it perfect," Niki added.

"It is, but I'm glad you guys called back. I need to talk."

"What's going on?" they both asked.

"I ran into Spencer in town today. He offered me an interesting proposition."

"What kind of proposition?" Niki asked hesitantly. Tia told them the general idea of what Spencer wanted her to do. "Are you going to do it?"

"I don't know yet…maybe. I'd be a fool to pass it up."

"I don't know Tia…" Nat began.

"I've been playing every possible scenario in my head. Still, doing the interview outweighs all my concerns. The boost to my career would be major. And right now I could seriously use it. It's not going as I expected."

"Wait, what do you mean, it's not going as you expected?"

"They pulled me off interviewing. I'm doing fluff pieces."

"Why didn't you tell us?"

"Because, it's my drama not yours," she said.

"What happened?"

"Right after the Istanbul incident, I went on an assignment to interview a corporate executive. He saw my on-air report and asked for me personally. It was a major get. I went in to do the interview and he wanted to trade for sex. When I refused and wrote the article anyway he decided to sue Global. Legal wants me off all interviewing until it's settled, which could be sometime in the next five years. Do you know what my career would be like after that? So, that's why getting an interview with Spencer would be so great."

"I have a better idea, why don't you interview David? He's got a movie coming out in a few months. The publicity machine is already starting up. His agent Lenny can set it up. I'll call…"

"No, Natalia, I'm not using your husband and my new brother-in-law like that."

"What do you mean? He'd love to do it. He loves doing interviews and you know he adores you."

"I know, but, no, I need to do this on my own."

"Well, what does Pam say?" Niki asked.

"I was going to call her in a few minutes and tell her."

"Tia, doing an interview requires you to get up close and personal, right."

"Right," Tia said.

"What about objectivity and distance. How can you keep them when the two of you have a physical history together? Isn't that considered a conflict of interest? And wouldn't it question your integrity just like with the corporate executive?" Niki asked.

"No, definitely not. I can compartmentalize and separate my personal life from my professional life. I do it all the time. I've interviewed dictators, degenerate rebels and even an accused terrorist. The only way news is supposed to work is if a reporter keeps personal feelings out of it."

"What if they blur? They did once before and look

what happened. Tia, you were devastated. Are you prepared to go through that again?" Nat asked.

"Nat, I need a change in my life. This opportunity couldn't have come at a better time. Doing Spencer's interview would put me back on top. He'd be my first interview in six months. It's a win-win situation. I'm here for a month. I can take care of the preliminaries while I'm here alone. It won't get personal."

"Are you sure, Tia? The last time you did an interview on Spencer was five years ago. Then Mason asked you to write his biography. After that all hell broke loose between you two."

"I know he broke my heart, but that's not happening this time. No one is ever getting that close to me again."

"I've seen you and Spencer together," Niki began. "You two have the chemistry. There's no way you're going to fight against that."

"I can't open my heart and give him my love again."

"Tia, love is something you've always wanted. I remember you're the one who always believed in fairy tales. If there's one thing I've learned, it's that you can't deny or run away from love. Love always has its own way in the end," Nat said.

"That worked for you. Not everybody walks down the aisle with their very own Prince Charming. I know Spencer. We go back a long time and—"

"No, and that's just it, you don't know him. You had a whirlwind romance. You were both head over heels in love. I don't think you just get over passion that strong. Just look at the other night."

Tia didn't say anything. Everything Nat and Niki were telling her she'd already thought about herself. But she knew she had to do this. It was her only way of getting back the reins on her career. "If all he wants is to win me back, then he's going to be disappointed. It won't work."

"Okay, just think carefully before you decide."

"I will. I'll text you tomorrow and let you know."

"Okay," they both said.

"It's still early, so I think I'm going to head down to the beach for a while before I start dinner."

"Sounds like a great idea," Niki said.

"Call us if you need us—anytime, okay?" Nat added.

"Yes, I will. I'll talk to you later. Bye."

Tia closed her cell and went back inside. She changed into her bathing suit then headed to the beach. As soon as she placed her towel on the chair and laid back, her cell phone rang again. It was Pam. "Hi, Pam, I was going to call you later, I've got some interesting news."

"So do I," she said.

"Okay, you first," Tia said.

Chapter 10

Tia lit the coals and watched a blazing fire reach for the night sky. She looked up at the billions of stars shining down on her. Suddenly, she felt insignificant and her problems were minuscule compared to the magnificent splendor of the universe. So what if her career was over. So what if the powers that be wanted to reassign her to the Germany office. So what if everything she worked for since college, her name, her reputation and her dreams, were all going up in a blaze just like the hibachi flame on the table in front of her.

Ordinarily she wouldn't just go out like this. She'd fight for what she knew was right, but she was too tired of all the drama. If she refused the new assignment, the company had grounds to fire her. She figured that's exactly what they expected her to do. She looked around again. Maybe she'd just stay here for the next year or so. Or better yet, maybe this was the perfect time to go to Madagascar and live on the beach like she always fantasized. She'd do a Hemingway and Baldwin and go all reclusive. She'd collect coconuts for a living and write lofty prose on them about life's miseries. Then she'd toss them into the Indian Ocean and wait for them to be discovered in about fifty years.

"Okay, *that* drama was way over the top," she said, chuckling to herself. Then she laughed out loud. The absurdity of it all would actually be funny if it wasn't so ridiculous. All this was because a man couldn't keep it in his pants. She chuckled again then got up and headed to the kitchen. She was preparing her favorite meal, so how bad could life really be right now?

Tonight she felt bohemian. She'd put on a strapless bikini and wrapped her hips low with a sheer matching scarf. She went barefoot with a heart charm on her ankle that jingled when she walked. Her hair was loose falling freely on her shoulders and she wore a long dangling chain around her neck.

To match her mood, she inserted her cell phone into the Bose system she found in the kitchen. She selected and set her playlist. Music began playing instantly. She stopped and listened for a while then turned to the refrigerator to retrieve the food for dinner. It was a slow sultry sound from a local group she heard while living in London. Their music was impossible to categorize.

It was jazz, it was rap and it was blues. It was also soul and hip-hop all mixed with a hot Latin flair. It set the perfect mood for what she was feeling.

She checked the counter, everything was cut up and ready to go. She picked up one of the wooden skewers she had soaking in water and was just about to thread shrimp on when her doorbell rang. She looked at the kitchen clock. It was after eight and she wasn't expecting anyone. She figured it was probably someone for the Sullivans. She quickly washed her hands, walked to the door and answered.

Spencer stood smiling with a fork in his hand. Then he stopped smiling as his gaze dropped. He didn't speak. His just stared down the length of her body. After a few seconds he looked back up into her face. He shook his head, amazed. The genuine admiration in his expression made her feel great. "My God, can you possibly get any more stunning than you are right now?"

"Thank you," she said as a warm blush touched her cheeks. "For that you get to come inside." She opened the door wider. He walked in with a bit of difficulty, she noted with a smile. Then, questioningly, she looked at the fork in his hand and then back at him. "So, what's up with the fork?" she asked.

"I'm starved. I burned my microwave dinner and ordering out takes too long. I remembered that Moroccan dish you told me about earlier, so I thought…"

"Let me guess. You thought you'd stop by and join

me for dinner," she said, finishing his sentence. "Don't you have a cook on staff?"

"I gave him the night off."

"What about cold cereal?"

"I couldn't find the milk."

"You don't drink milk."

"That's probably why I couldn't find any."

She shook her head chuckling. He tried to look sincerely pitiful. It didn't work. But, she gave in anyway. Maybe company was exactly what she needed. "Sure, why not? Your timing's perfect. The grill's almost ready. I was just about to put the food on." She turned and began walking to the kitchen. He watched. "How are you at grilling?" she tossed over her shoulder.

He took a deep breath and blew out shaking his head. He wasn't sure he was going to get through the night. He knew walking would be a problem at the moment. "Do you even have to ask?" he challenged back to her. Then he followed her to the kitchen at a reasonable distance and with great difficulty.

"Okay, you have grill duty," she said circling the counter.

He placed a brown paper bag on the kitchen table. "I brought dessert," he said.

"I hope there's no ice cream melting in the bag."

"Nah, not this time. I learned my lesson."

"So, what's for dessert?" she asked looking at the bag.

"I'll tell you after dinner," he said secretively. She

nodded and then began skewering the shrimp while he washed his hands. "Okay, where do you want me?"

"Outside," she said.

"Hmm, you want me outside. I like the sound of that," he teased.

She looked up and shook her head. He was incorrigible. "The hibachi is outside. You can check and see if the coals are ready. I'll be out in a minute with the food."

He opened the sliding door and stepped outside. Tia watched him go. As soon as he closed the screen door behind him, she exhaled. He looked too good in just jeans and a T-shirt. And heaven help her, whatever cologne he was wearing should be marketed as an aphrodisiac or love potion number one.

She grabbed the iced tea she made earlier and poured two classes. She took a long sip from one of the glasses. The ice-cold liquid flowed down her throat with sweetened ease. She needed that. But it only did so much to cool her insides. She was still burning for him. She quickly finished with the vegetables and seafood then headed outside with a tray.

Spencer turned and watched her approach. He smiled. She was absolutely mouthwatering. The outfit she wore was sexy and totally enticing. He longed to touch her, knowing her smooth skin would be just as luxurious as the material she wore.

She placed a tray on the outside table and walked over to the grill. "Perfect. Are you ready to eat?"

He smiled. "I'm always ready to eat."

She ignored his remark. Picking up several skewers and placing them on the grill. "Okay, shrimp, halibut and snapper—it's all yours. I'll be inside finishing the couscous and sauce." She hurried inside and busied herself making seasoned pasta and cutting fruit and nuts to mix in. Fifteen minutes later she returned. The aromas wafting from the grill area were absolutely delectable. "Mmm, it smells delicious over there," she said, carrying another tray to the table. This time she had a covered dish and two glasses on it.

He turned and hurried over to help her with the tray. As he reached, their hands touched. She looked up at him. "I'll take that for you," he said softly. She nodded and he took the tray, placing it on the table. He went to open the covered dish but she stopped him.

"No, don't open it yet. It's not quite ready," she said, handing him a glass of iced tea instead. "I didn't expect company tonight. All I have is sweetened iced tea."

"Sounds good to me," he said taking the glass and drinking half the tea in one long swallow. "Mmm, that's good."

"I'm gonna go get the plates and silverware. I planned on sitting out here on the terrace tonight, do you mind?"

"No, not at all. It's the perfect setting—the stars, the moonlight and you," he said softly. "I don't know what's more amazing to me. Being here with you tonight or having you back in my life. Do you have any idea what you do to me?"

"Okay, you can stop with the pick-up lines," she quipped.

He shook his head slowly as he gazed deep into her eyes. "Trust me, believe me, that wasn't a pick-up line," he said in all honesty, surprising even himself. "I need you, Tatiana. No matter what happened, know that you will always have my heart."

She looked at him and smiled silently. That was the problem, she believed him too much. He wasn't making this easy. "I gotta…um, I gotta get the table stuff," she stammered and muttered, knowing that instant she was desperately in love all over again.

She went back inside and grabbed the iced tea pitcher and held it tight. The cold sweating ice cooled her trembling hands, but not her hopeful heart. She paused for a moment and focused her thinking. If she was going to do this interview, she had to separate personal from business. She knew she could do it. She did it all the time. But it would be crazy to think this was going to be easy. She was in love with Spencer. She placed her ice cold hand on her face, neck and chest. The chill cooled her skin for just a short minute.

She turned and looked outside. Spencer was standing across the terrace looking in at her. With the muted darkness outside and the bright lighting in the kitchen, he saw every move she made. Just then her cell phone rang. It was still sitting in the music system on the kitchen counter. She glanced at the displayed caller ID and saw who was calling then let it go to voice mail.

She held up the pitcher. "Would you like some more iced tea?"

"Sure, sounds good," he called back.

She nodded and opened the screen door and went back outside with the tea, plates and silverware. She began setting the table then glanced back only once to see Spencer totally focused on his chore. One of her favorite songs played. Without thinking, she began humming and softly singing the chorus.

Spencer smiled as she sang. He shook his head tortuously. He knew he had to do this, but his heart was breaking more and more. Their first night together sealed his fate. He would betray her and cause her the worst pain imaginable. He would destroy their love and live the rest of his life knowing he'd sacrificed his heart to save his life's work. He had to do this. He had no choice. The alternative was unthinkable. He turned to her. She smiled peacefully as she lit the lanterns. He had to do this.

A few minutes later he finished with the food on the grill. He brought the platter of skewered vegetables and seafood to the table. Tia had set it beautifully with cloth napkins, flowers and lanterns for added illumination. She stood at the end of the table stirring something into the lidded dish. "Okay, I'm all set with the grilled food," he said.

"And the couscous is ready, too. Let's eat." She served their plates as he poured more tea into their glasses. They ate with rousing gusto, talking and laughing about everything under the sun. When the meal was finished and they cleared the plates to the kitchen, they sat chatting about his music while still listening to hers.

"This group is really pretty good. Who are they?" he asked.

She told him their name and what she knew about them. She'd done a freelance article of the hidden treasures of London and they were one of her finds. "Who reps them?" he asked.

"No one as far as I know," she said. "They have a CD out, but they don't seem to do it for the money or the fame. It's all about the sound and the feeling. They're amazing."

"Yes, they are. Maybe I should contact them. What do you think?"

"I think they'll be a hard sell. But they'd be thrilled to meet you. You know they live in London."

"Yeah, so…?"

"So, I thought you couldn't go to London—some kind of legal issue."

"That wasn't me, that was Mason. The rest of us decided never to go in solidarity."

She grimaced. "Are you sure?" she asked. He nodded.

"That's not what he told me."

"What did he tell you?"

"He told me you couldn't go there because of a legal matter involving a woman."

Spencer laughed. "No, that was definitely Mason.

He got into a fight with some guy over the guy's wife. The Bobbies were called and his visa was revoked. Apparently the guy he beat up was the son of a member of Parliament."

"Why would he intentionally tell me something different?"

"Maybe you just misunderstood," he surmised.

"Yeah, maybe," she nodded, but she knew she didn't. It looked like Mason deliberately lied to her. This wasn't the first time she found out he had lied to her about something. Writing his biography was nearly impossible. The fact-checking took almost as long as actually writing the book. She still wasn't sure what that was all about.

"Ready for dessert?" he asked, standing up.

"I think I'm more curious. What is it?"

"I'll be right back." He went into the kitchen while she stayed outside. While getting the bag, her cell phone rang again. He looked down, seeing the caller ID. It was Donavan. A muscle in his jaw twitched. Whatever he was going to do, he needed to do it fast. He went back outside with the brown paper bag. He opened it and pulled out a bottle of wine, several bars of milk chocolate candy, graham crackers and marshmallows.

She smiled. "S'mores."

"Yes. The hibachi is still hot. Would you like one?"

"Sure, why not? I'd love a s'more."

She threaded a few marshmallows onto some skewers while he opened and poured the wine into two plastic cups. She handed him one of the long wooden sticks, then they went over to the hibachi. They laughed and talked about the last time they each had s'mores while their marshmallows heated through and the insides became soft and pliable. Hers caught fire twice. Afterward they went back to the table of assembled the dessert and ate. The result was a sweet, gooey delicacy they both enjoyed.

They'd just finished making their second s'more when a heavy sonic boom broke the stilled calmness of the night. Tia tensed in her seat and dropped her dessert. She looked around panicky. A high-pitched squeal sounded and a heavy crack split the sky. A blast of light shot above their heads then sparked into a glittering crystal orb and sprinkled down like sparkling jewels.

"Hey, hey, relax," Spencer said, leaning close and seeing Tia's fluster, "it's just fireworks." She turned around and looked up, seeing the sky sparkle and sprinkle down like dazzling crystals. "Are you okay?"

She nodded breathlessly. "Yes, loud unexpected noises sometimes make me tense," she said in understatement. Actually, loud unexpected noises horrified her.

He stood and held his hand out to her. "Come here," he said. She took his hand and stood. He wrapped his arms around her body and hugged her close. "Leftovers from Istanbul?" he said.

"Yeah, that and for the first two weeks a constant ringing in my ears. But that's gone now. I'm just a little jumpy when I hear sudden loud noises. They say I had acute stress reaction, but I'm a lot better now."

"I can definitely understand that. What you experienced was unimaginable." He squeezed her tight. His heart trembled recalling his own memory of the event. There was no way he could tell her that he stayed in front of the television the whole time she was reporting. Then when a second explosion went off and her news feed was disconnected he made desperate arrangements to head straight to Istanbul. All flights were grounded, so he was just about to hire a private jet. Then her report resumed. He was never so happy to see her face as he was that moment. "My uncle has PTSD, posttraumatic stress disorder, from his years in Vietnam. He doesn't like loud thunder or fireworks."

"Your uncle? Wow, first you talk about your father and now your uncle. I'm impressed. You're really opening up."

"Don't get too used to it," he joked.

They walked to the edge of the terrace and stood looking up at the wondrous sight. The brilliance of the spectacular display was infectious. The sky exploded again. She jumped. He held tight. An array of shimmering colors rained down. People still out on the beach began applauding. The show continued with breathtaking wonder. Each time there was the earth-rumbling sound followed by the thin slit in the darkness and afterward a blast of color and radiance.

Spencer stepped behind Tia and wrapped his arms

around her body and held her close. Their bodies tucked into a perfect mold. When it looked as if the firework display had finished, they stood remaining in the same position. She turned slightly and looked up at him. He seemed pensive and troubled, just like he did in the magazine photo. "Are you okay?"

"Oh, yeah, I'm good," he said. She nodded and then turned back to the sky. "You know, sometimes I think about the night we met and I wonder."

"Wonder about what?" she asked looking up at him again.

"You were interviewing Mason and writing an article on BoomBox. Man, I looked at you that first moment and I swear my heart stopped beating. I knew, I knew right then," he said, then looked away and shook his head. "What would have happened if we'd stayed together five years ago when we first met? How would our lives have been different? Would we be the same two people we are now?"

She shook her head. "No, I don't think so. It's our experiences that make us who we are." She smiled. "I had no idea who you were at the time, but I knew you were something special."

"We talked until dawn that first night," he reminisced.

She chuckled shaking her head. "That's not all we did that first night. It was crazy. I remember we made love then watched sunrise from the roof while a jam-packed party was going on downstairs. I still can't believe I did that after just meeting you."

He smiled as the memory touched his heart. "I know, but there was something so perfect about us being together that night. It was almost scary. It was like we'd known each other all our lives, but we were complete strangers. We fit. We made sense. We connected. We still do."

"We also walked away from each other," she said.

They went silent for a few minutes as both looked up at the stars. "Then we met up again when you were writing the bio for Mason. I thought it was fate bringing you back into my life, but then…"

"…we walked away again."

He nodded. "Now, here we are again, years later. Being here with you right now is what was supposed to happen five years ago, but we keep messing it up. Is this ever going to happen for us?"

She stepped out of his embrace. "Maybe we're just supposed to be friends," she said.

He smiled. "No, you don't believe that any more than I do. We need to hold on this time, no matter what happens." He reached out and took her hand and gently pulled her back into his embrace. He wrapped his arm around her body and pressed her close. They started moving to the music in their hearts. The slow, sweet sway of his body made her body burn. Her heart pounded and her stomach quivered.

She reached up and caressed his neck as she dipped

her head into the curve of his shoulder. "Why are you doing this to me?"

He leaned back and looked into her eyes. "Doing what?" he asked cautiously.

"Making me want you again," she said.

"No, you have that the wrong way 'round."

"Spencer, about the interview you'd like me to do…"

"No, don't give me your answer now. Think about it some more. In the meantime, come with me tomorrow to Nantucket."

"Nantucket?" she said.

"Just say yes. I'm not leaving until noon. I'll come by around eleven-thirty. Think about it, and then do it anyway." He leaned down and kissed her cheek then spoke softly in her ear. "Thank you for dinner tonight. I had a wonderful evening. I'd better go before we…"

Tia closed her eyes, feeling the tender softness of his lips on her skin. She wanted more, needed more. But she knew opening this door would lead her down a path that could never end well. How do you fight for your heart when all your heart wants to do is surrender to love? He turned to head back to the house. He walked across the terrace and got to the porch steps.

The word left her mouth before she thought. "Spencer."

He turned to meet her eyes. She took a deep breath then walked over to him. They stood face-to-face, chest to chest. "I need to know—what is this really about? What do you want from me?" she asked.

He smiled and gently stroked the side of her face. "Sweetheart, don't you know? I want it all, everything, starting right here." He let his fingers drift down her neck to her shoulder then over to the chest. He stopped at her heart.

"This can't be right. We've tried this twice before."

"No, not like this. Besides, third time's a charm."

She was speechless. For the first time in a long time words failed her. Her heart and her emotions were taking over. Wanting him was easy, keeping her heart intact, wasn't. But right now she needed him just one more time. She slowly pulled his T-shirt from his jeans, then high above his head. When it was free from his body she tossed it on the padded swing behind him. She unzipped his jeans feeling the stone hardness of his penis press against the back of her hand. He groaned as she touched him. She couldn't look up. Seeing him would break the spell.

She nibbled her lower lip, busying herself removing the rest of his clothes. When she was done and he was naked she looked down at his body. He was magnificent—hard and ready. She began kissing him everywhere, even there. He groaned. "Tatiana," he breathed in almost a rumbling purr. She placed her hand on his chest and maneuvered him to step back. The padded swing was deep and wide, easily comfortable for two and perfect for what she had in mind.

"Do you have any condoms?"

"My pocket," he said.

She grabbed it from his jeans as he sat down. She stepped closer, straddled his legs to sit on his lap. He held her waist, stroking her thighs, hips, her arms and her back. She caressed his shoulders and chest, almost fascinated by the feel of his body. His skin was hot. She gently scratched and raked her nails along the curves and muscles in his arms. She heard him take a deep breath and watched his chest expand. She felt her bikini top loosen. She looked up. His eyes were half closed and a muscle in his neck strained, tightened and flinched.

He placed his hands on her breasts and massaged them until her nipples hardened. Her body quivered as he pulled her closer and licked her nipples. She gasped, inching back, but his hand kept her in place. His torturous tongue and magnificent mouth licked, nibbled and devoured her. Her thoughts muddled as she felt him untie the scarf and release the side snap holding her bikini bottom in place. The swing swayed slowly as she sat up and adjusted her position, instantly feeling the hardness of his penis beneath her. He leaned back and pulled her close down onto his body. She closed her eyes savoring the feelings. The tip of his penis was just at her core.

Then he lifted her and pressed her to lie down. He spread her legs over his shoulders. She knew what he intended to do. "Spencer, come inside."

"I will, but first I want to taste you." He leaned down and licked her with the flat of his tongue. She gasped loudly. "Mmm, you taste delicious." He licked her again, this time slower and more deliberate. Her legs trembled. "Yes, I want something from you, Tatiana. Will you give me what I want?" She didn't answer. She couldn't, her mind was awash with sensual pleasure. He used the tip of his tongue next and then he devoured her. She writhed and squealed, near sexual madness. "Are you ready for me?"

"Yes. Yes. Yes," she said breathlessly.

He pulled her to sit up on his lap again. That instant she felt it. The thickness of his penis was right at her clitoris. His tip was there. He thrust upward and entered her. Her stomach jumped and every nerve ending in her body tightened.

"Open your eyes," he whispered.

She did.

"Now, move your hips," he mouthed without speaking.

She did. She rocked her body. Over and over again she gyrated her hips as the swing swayed in response. The slow seductive rhythm began to increase as the motion of the swing matched the movements of her body.

She sat up even straighter as her speed increased. Then she arched and leaned back with one hand on his knee and the other on his shoulder. The pace was now frantic as she thrust her body onto him. She watched him watch her. Her body writhed and squirmed as her coming pleasure advanced. He thrust to penetrate deeper. She felt him all through her body. Then she shuddered and trembled. Her nails bit into his shoulder. Her climax surged. She closed her eyes and opened her mouth.

A sudden burst erupted inside of her. She held her breath, feeling the heightened explosion coming. She held tight to her release as she felt his body tense also. He thrust, then gripped her tight. A rush of spectacular sensations flashed through their bodies. She trembled in ecstasy. The intensity of the orgasm was beyond words. She shook all over. He thrust his hips against her body once more. She gasped, screamed then climaxed again. Moments later she collapsed against him. He held her tight in his loving embrace. She closed her eyes and laid her head on his shoulder while her heart raced.

When she opened her eyes a few hours later she realized she was still outside and she wasn't alone. Spencer was still there. He had laid down on the swing and cuddled her in his arms. His breathing was calm and even, but she knew he wasn't asleep. "Hey," she said stirring slightly. "You're awake."

"Yes, I'm awake," he confirmed softly.

"I guess I passed out."

"You talk in your sleep now. That's new."

"What did I say?"

"Nothing much," he lied.

"What time is it?" she asked.

"Late or early," he answered. "Either way, I probably need to get home."

She sat up, then stood and looked down at her body

realizing she was wearing his T-shirt and nothing else. She looked back at him as he sat up and stood. He had his pants on. The bottom hem of his T-shirt reached just to her cheeks. He couldn't help but admire it. "It looks good on you."

"Thanks, I'll get it back to you."

"Don't worry about it."

He walked over to where she stood with her back to him and wrapped his arms around her body. He reached down between her legs and moaned. She gasped and wiggled. He held her tight dipping his finger inside of her. "I can't get enough of you," he said kissing her neck. "I love tasting you and watching you come." He dipped into her again as his other hand massaged her breast. He tantalized her tiny pleasure. She began breathing harder then reached up, wrapping her arms around his neck for balance. Moments later she twitched in silent pleasure giving him exactly what he wanted. "Remind me to do that with a mirror next time."

He held her and they stood awhile longer. Then he took her hand and walked back inside to the front door. Neither spoke. He opened the door and turned to her. "Nantucket. I hope I see you later today. Good night, Tatiana."

"Good night, Spencer."

Chapter 11

The run on the beach the next morning was exactly what Tia needed. It was just after dawn when she started out, just a few hours after she'd gone to bed. The beach was mostly empty at this time of morning. There were a few other runners out and several people in and at the water's edge with surfboards. Several older men roamed the beach with metal detectors intent on finding treasure. She listened to her music as she headed to the far point lighthouse. When she got there she stopped and walked around while stretching her legs. She was stiff and her legs burned. It had been a while since she ran and apparently she was more out of condition than she thought. Still slightly breathless, she turned around and looked back to where she'd come from. The cottage was almost two miles away.

The run had sparked her energy level after another sleepless night. Although, she was surprised her not sleeping had more to do with Spencer than her usual nightmares. After he left, she slept for a short time, then showered and changed and went back outside on the back porch for a while. The fireworks display had long since ended and the beach below was quiet and still. The sound of cascading waves on sand lulled her to peaceful memories.

She had gazed up at the stars searching for the three that always centered her. Together, Alnika, Alnilam and Mintaka made up Orion's belt. From there she found Betelgeuse and Rigel. Then the full constellation, Orion with his bow drawn back in archer's stance, emerged.

Orion, The Hunter, was the most prominent in the sky and her favorite constellation. It was located on the celestial equator and visible from all over the world. No matter where she went on assignment, as soon as she looked up at the night sky and saw Orion, she felt close to everything she knew and loved. She smiled at the memory. Spencer once pointed out the main constellations to her. It was the first night they met.

It was the beginning of everything for her. Just out of college, her life and career had taken the fast track as soon as they met. It started as a simple fact-finding assignment for an article her magazine was doing. Then Mason was so impressed, he told the magazine he wanted her to do the interview, as well. She met Spencer at a BoomBox party. He was surrounded by women. He glanced at her and walked over and every-thing changed. They were inseparable. And now it was starting all over again.

She thought about her answer all morning. He had offered her a huge opportunity. Securing and doing the interview could change everything. It would make a deep impact on her career, but she knew she'd be asking for trouble if she did it.

After everything that happened between them over the years, he was still too easy to love. And she did love him. Their first evening together made it clear. Last night made it expressly understood. She couldn't keep putting her heart at risk. They'd had their chance before, but then again, what if this time was the right time.

Her cell phone music paused. She was getting a text. She slowed her pace and pulled her phone from her pocket. She read the text and stopped running. It was from Pam. Pam had told Greer, her boss, about the in-terview and he was thrilled. He couldn't wait to see the preliminary pages.

"Oh, no," she muttered. "No." She quickly called Pam. She answered on the first ring. "Pam, good morn-ing, it's Tatiana. I just got your text message."

"Isn't it fantastic? I just got off the phone with Greer again this morning. Don't you just love that London is six hours ahead? He already met with the entertain-ment division at Global. They're thrilled. He's taking the lead on this and you're at point. Apparently Spencer

Cage is an impossible get, but you got him. Needless to say Greer couldn't stop raving about you. He seemed to think the reason you didn't go to Paris was you had an inside line on Spencer Cage."

"I wonder how he got that idea," Tia said.

"Guilty. But I didn't lie. I only gave him the facts. He jumped to his own conclusions. Well, maybe I pushed just a little. Anyway, he's putting the whole thing in motion from his side. I think the contract has already gone out."

"Pam, I didn't agree to do it."

"How can you not? This is a golden opportunity handed to you on a platinum platter. Spencer Cage is a business icon who's been out of circulation for years. Anyone getting his first interview out would be thrilled. And the fact that he's asking for you personally is a cherry on top."

"We have a history."

"Great, then you already have a sense of his personality."

"We have a romantic history," Tia clarified.

"Fine, you'll separate it and still do a fantastic job."

"I haven't told him I'd do it."

"Tatiana, this is your ticket back in. Take it. Do it."

"I'll talk to you later, Pam."

"Wait, one more thing. I don't know if you already know this but there are rumors that his company will be getting bought by a larger record label soon. If that happens you'll be right there to get the scoop."

"Where did you hear that?"

"Greer told me."

This was all getting too big. Greer knew about the interview offer and now the entertainment division at Global knew about it. She didn't have much choice now. She had to do it. She looked at the time on her cell phone. She needed to pick up some items in town if she was going to do this. She started running again. To her surprise it took her far less time to get back to the cottage than she expected. She showered, dressed, tossed a few things into a suitcase and hurried out. She had a few stops to make before catching a boat to Nantucket.

Spencer spent the morning rechecking the rigging and getting everything ready for the trip to Nantucket. He had gone to the boat early for his usual pre-sail check. When he finished looking over the standing rigging, he checked the wires, ropes, shackles and pins. He double-checked the halyard and sheet lines, securing all the leads so that they were free from knots, snags and obstructions. The boom swung wide. He grabbed it and held tight then pulled all lines free of winches and cleats, making sure they were all clear and moved freely.

He rolled and secured the gybe, then wrapped it firmly. Then he took down the main silk and checked it. He filled the main engine, mindful he had a readily available backup power source. He tested and turned the engine on. Everything checked out securely. He went down below and made sure the supplies he ordered the day before had been placed onboard and all free-standing items were secured. When everything was prepared to his satisfaction, he headed back to his house to grab his bags and pick up Tia.

At eleven thirty he stopped by the Sullivan's cottage exactly as he promised. He rang the doorbell and waited patiently for Tia to answer. A few minutes later he rang it a second then third time. There was still no answer. He knocked then walked around to the back of the small structure. The area showed no signs of the wonderful evening they had the night before. He continued to where the hibachi sat on the raised stone platform. The cold embers of charcoal had been cleared and disposed of. He looked back at the house. It was like the night before never happened. He continued over to the top of the steps leading to the beach. Tia was nowhere in sight.

Disappointed, he went back to his car and drove to the docks. For the first time in a long time he took his time. He was in no particular hurry. When he finally got to the docks he unloaded his bags from the trunk and locked his car, then headed to his boat. As soon as he walked up he saw a woman in white shorts and a navy blue striped top sitting up on the rail. Her head was turned and she was looking out to sea, but he knew exactly who it was. He smiled instantly. Her hair, in loose curls that blew in the light breeze, was pulled back with a white hair band. Seeing her waiting for him made his heart soar.

She turned to him and smiled as he approached. He was gorgeous. White shirt and shorts with boat shoes and baseball cap. "Good afternoon," she said, as she slid down from the rail.

He reached out to steady her as her feet touched the wooden planks. "Good afternoon," he said then leaned in and kissed her long and lovingly. "I'm glad you decided to come with me."

"Me, too," she said.

"You look beautiful, very nautical."

"Thank you." She blushed then glanced at the large boat behind her. "So, this is it, huh?"

"Yep, it is," he said, looking at her instead of the boat.

"Do I have to call you Captain Cage?" she asked.

"Only if you want to," he joked.

She turned and tipped her head up to the height of the mast. "It's a lot bigger than it looked yesterday. Are you sure you got this?"

"I'll take very good care of you, I promise. Now, are you ready to get started?"

She nodded smiling. "Yeah, I'm ready."

"Let's go."

"Okay. What do you need me to do?"

"Have you ever sailed before?"

"On my brother's boat, but he has a fishing cruiser. It looks a lot different from this. So what can I do to help?"

"Nothing, just sit back and enjoy the ride."

He stored everything onboard while she stayed top deck taking pictures. As he came back up, she took his picture. His smile was candid and genuine. She sat and watched as he busied himself preparing to launch the boat. There was another man who came on board to help. They maneuvered the sloop away from the dock, the helper waved, then hopped off. In no time they were gliding through the water leaving the harbor behind. When they cleared the other boats the excitement really began.

Spencer pointed the boat into the wind as he raised the jib sail under minimal resistance. There was a mild wind, so they sailed in calm waters. After the flurry of activity to get the boat underway, there was a nice, easy lull. Spencer held the wheel and steered the boat farther out to sea. Tia looked around in awe. The water was a blue-gray and the sky was a brilliant blue with the midday sun shining bright. The horizon, one continuous line, cut the two in half. Tia looked behind her. The Martha's Vineyard coastline was farther then she expected. It had nearly vanished. "How do you know which way we're going?"

"I have charts and even GPS instruments. Also, I've sailed to Nantucket many times. I know the way."

"How long will it take?"

"It's about ten miles, so it usually doesn't take that long, depending on the currents and wind. But I thought we'd circle the island first, so it'll be a little longer."

"How fast are we going now?"

He checked his instruments. "We have a good twenty knot wind. So we're doing around ten or twelve knots but the current's a little choppy. We'll be approaching the Nantucket Sound in a few minutes. You'll see Muskeget Island on the starboard." She stood and looked to the left. He smiled as she looked around to the wrong side of the boat. "Your other starboard, over there, to the right."

They passed a small patch of land. "Is that it?" she asked, pointing across the water. He nodded. She got up and carefully walked back to where he stood. "So Nantucket is next, right?"

"Tuckernuck Island is next, and then we'll sail past Nantucket in a few minutes."

"Sail past it?" she queried.

"We're sailing around Nantucket to the western end going to Madaket Harbor. There was low tide this morning, so I'm hoping we can get in now. But with shifting sands, who knows. As long as we don't go hard aground and bang the rudder we'll be fine."

"What?"

"I'm joking. I'm joking. We're fine." He chuckled.

"Not funny."

After a while they came to, and then passed a larger mass of land. "Was that Nantucket?" she asked.

"Yes. Are you ready for some fun?"

She looked at him. There was a twinkle in his eyes. Her adventurous spirit immediately surged. "Yes."

"Okay, let's do it." He double-checked everything

then readied to hoist the mainsail. He pulled the halyard down until it stopped. It flailed and flapped wildly. He tightened the luff, freeing the folds. He tied off the winch then raised the front sail by pulling the halyard and securing it. He pulled down on another rope and the larger mainsail rose to the top of the mast. The wind took the mainsail.

The boat jerked then took off instantly. Everything loose fluttered and waved. Moments later they were skimming the top and cutting through the water like a flying arrow to a bull's eye. The rushing sound of wind gusts kept constant, nearly taking her breath away. They seemed to be flying. The speed was thrilling and intense. Tia couldn't believe they were going so fast. The wind in her face felt fantastic. She felt free and unbound by anything. She held tight, watching as Spencer turned the large steering wheel.

The boat tipped nearly to its side as it was set right into the wind. The sails flapped wildly and the boom swung wide then stopped. The boat went up then splashed down and a wave crashed into its side. They did it again and again, bouncing like a ball on the waves. She squealed and laughed as a spray of salted water splashed them repeatedly. She shrieked gleefully. She was soaked and loving it. He turned the wheel, ending their wild ride. "Oh, my God, that was awesome."

He laughed. Her reaction was priceless. "Do you want to give it a try?"

"No way, I'll capsize us."

"Trust me you won't. Just stand up and grab your wheel." She stood and took the other wheel beside his. "Are you ready?" he asked. She nodded hesitantly. He flipped a switch, then let go. She controlled the boat. She squealed again, laughing hysterically. "Turn it a little to the right," he called out. She did. The wind caught the sail and the boat took off again. A few minutes later he stood behind her with his hands on her wheel with her. "Now turn to the left a little bit." She did. The wind released the sail and they glided effortlessly.

"Okay, enough, enough," she called out over her shoulder. "Take the wheel." He did. She sat down and watched him. He was a natural. He was focused and confident. The intense look in his eyes as he controlled the boat was chilling. She grabbed her camera and took his picture. He never turned her way. She doubted he even realized she took it. She wanted everyone to see the man she saw. She made her decision. She was going to do the interview. After a while she looked around. There was nothing but horizon line all around them. "Where are we? There's no land."

"We're about nine miles east of Nantucket."

"You mean in the middle of the Atlantic Ocean?"

"Not exactly in the middle of the ocean, the distance between New York and Europe is over three thousand miles, but…"

"Doesn't matter, I need to see some land."

He laughed. "Okay, sounds good to me, too. Are

you hungry?" She nodded. "Good let's get something to eat."

He turned the boat and sailed back to Nantucket. They skirted the coast with only the drifters sail and then glided easily into Madaket Harbor. He lowered and secured the sails. They pulled into the channel and headed to a private dock. A man and woman waved from the upper deck as they approached. The woman stayed where she was, but the man started down to the lower deck. "Friends?" Tia asked.

"No, family," he said.

"You're taking me to meet your family?" she said.

"Yes, my mom and dad." He waved back just as the man reached the dock. The man continued coming toward the boat. Spencer tossed a rope to shore. The man caught it and pulled tight as Spencer bumped the side of the boat against the thick rubber padding. "Hi, Dad," he called out.

The other man hopped onboard and helped secure the boat. They hugged and shook hands then turned and smiled at Tia. "Well, now, who do we have here?"

"Dad, this is Tatiana Coles, a very good friend. Tia, this is Elwood Jackson."

"It's a pleasure meeting you, sir."

"Good to meet you, too, Tatiana. Please, call me Elwood. Come on up to the house, lunch is just about ready."

Tia was still too shocked. Spencer had brought her to meet his parents. She couldn't believe it. They got out and headed up toward the house with Elwood and Spencer carrying their bags. The woman who waved earlier greeted them as they approached the top deck. Spencer hurried in front and gave her a long hug then turned around. "Mom, this is Tatiana Coles, a very good friend. Tia, this is Claire Jackson."

"Hello, Tatiana, nice to meet you."

"You, too. It's a pleasure, Mrs. Jackson."

"Call me Claire, please. I know you're hungry after being on that boat. You didn't scare Tatiana to death, did you?"

"We had fun," Spencer admitted.

"Good Lord, that's what I'm afraid of. Come on up to the house. Lunch is just about ready."

They headed to the house, which was a sweet country-styled post-and-beam bungalow a little larger than the Sullivan's cottage. Since Tia and Spencer were still damp from the boat ride, they freshened up and changed then joined the couple out on the terrace. Lunch consisted of a seafood and steak surf and turf feast. They steamed and grilled outside and then sat in a screened gazebo eating and enjoying the warm sea breeze. Claire and Elwood told stories about their life together and also about Spencer as a child and his passion for music.

Later, just as dusk approached, the Jacksons headed inside for the evening, leaving Spencer and Tia alone. They stayed out on the terrace talking. Then later they went for a walk down to the dock. He lead her to the lower deck and then down to the beach. They stood in the soft sand in silence, watching the reflection of the sun setting on the water. The vibrant colors shimmered and lit up the surface, seeming to set it ablaze. It was a stunning sight. "It's so beautiful here," she whispered.

"I know it's not Madagascar, but…"

"It's perfect. Thank you for inviting me."

"I'm glad you came."

"Me, too," she said looking into his eyes. "I feel so good here with you right now."

"*Good,* is that all?" he asked, hoping for more.

"Right now, good is everything there is." She touched his face, reached up and kissed him. What she intended to be a sweet, loving gesture of intimacy instantly turned into ravaging desire. The kiss exploded. When it finally ended he touched her face then ran his hand down the front of her body.

The top she wore fastened with fours ties in front. He pulled the first one loose. The shirt gapped slightly, exposing the top swell of her breasts. He quickly pulled the second, third and fourth free. Her shirt hung open but still covered her breasts. She watched a muscle in his jaw tighten and clench. His face was tense and focused as he gently fingered the top tie. "I've wanted to do that all evening," he confessed.

"Funny, I've wanted to do this." She unzipped his pants and stroked his penis through the material. He was already hard. She heard his breathing quicken. Smiling, she reached down and held him tighter. His body quivered. He leaned in and kissed her neck and tweaked her nipple as she continued to stroke his throbbing penis. He grabbed her rear and pressed her closer. She closed her eyes and gasped, then held his head to her body.

"Wait, wait a minute," he gasped breathlessly, stopping her hand. "I don't have a condom here. We need to get to the boat." Still holding her hand he turned to walk. She didn't move. He turned to look at her in wonder. She smiled and pulled a condom from her skirt pocket.

He smiled. "I love you."

"No horizontal promises."

He shook his head. "It wasn't."

She wasn't sure what he meant, but right now she was sure what she wanted, *him.* She opened the packet and pulled out the condom, careful not to get sand on it. She looked around for an obscure place. He pulled her to a covered grassy knoll a few feet away beneath a covering of low hanging branches. She removed her long skirt and panties then watched as he undressed, as well. He took the condom from her and covered his enormous manhood. Then he lay down on his back bringing her on top of him.

She impaled herself. The thickness and length of his penis filled her completely. He sat up and held her rear in place. She wrapped her arms around his neck and began to move her hips. She plunged and thrust in a wavelike motion. Unrestrained passions exploded as kissing, licking and biting quickened her pace to a frantic need. She arched back. He devoured her breasts and nipples. She gasped breathlessly as shrieks of passion intensified. He held her tight, still her legs weakened and wobbled. She felt it coming. Her heart raced and every nerve in her body tensed. Wave after wave, she climbed higher and higher, closer and closer. Then she reached her crest. She nearly screamed. Her body stiffened and shook.

Seconds later she realized he was still hard inside of her. She lifted up and plunged down onto his body again. A second climax shot through her. She slowly gyrated and grinded against him, feeling her strength gradually return. She began again. Moments later she felt his body tense. She plunged harder and quicker. He gripped her hips to slow the pace, but she wouldn't let up. She knew his release to coming. He exploded and bucked, lurching up high, taking her with him. When he sat back down, they held each other in a wordless embrace.

Chapter 12

The next three days on Nantucket Island were joyful and exhilarating. They went bicycling, fishing, sailing and, interspersed between all the outside activities, they shopped in nearly every boutique and antique store on the Island. In the evenings they'd have a quiet dinner with his family or dine in one of the many local restaurants in town. Coincidentally, there were two popular annual events going on while they were there, the Annual August Antique Show and the ACK Nantucket Race Week.

They extended their stay another day to attend the beginning of Race Week, a weeklong celebration of waters sports, regattas and parties. The first day was also Spencer's birthday. To celebrate, they all hung out on the boat watching races until sunset. Tia was surprised how much fun she was having. Afterward, she and Claire cooked a delicious dinner that included chocolate cupcakes and homemade French vanilla ice cream for dessert.

When Claire presented the cupcakes with the scoop of slightly melted frozen delight, Spencer looked at Tia and smiled. She knew exactly what he was thinking. Later they all visited the local street party, then relaxed with a quiet evening at the house. The next day they prepared to leave. They said their goodbyes, then sailed around the island one last time before heading back to Martha's Vineyard.

Tia relaxed back on the rear cushions and watched Spencer at the wheel. The ride was smooth and tranquil. She couldn't help but admire Spencer's proficiency at the wheel. "You're really very good at this," she said admiringly.

"Thanks. I don't get to sail as much as I'd like. Business takes most of my time. So when I'm out on the water I love it. It makes me feel free."

"Have you ever been out when the weather's really bad?"

"Oh, yes, a few times. I've been out in the rain, the fog and one really horrendous thunderstorm. I've seen the waves range everywhere from eight feet high to as smooth and flat as glass."

"Are you going to enter Race Week one year?"

"Maybe. I hope so, but I'll need a crew."

She laughed, imagining Drill, Donavan and Riley working the boats like some of the men and women she saw at the regatta. "I don't think the guys are up for the challenge."

He turned to her. "Actually I was talking about you."

She blushed. "All the way from London? That's kind of far to crew a boat, don't you think?"

"Perhaps if I asked, you'd move back to the States."

"I guess anything's possible," she said suggestively, leaving her exact meaning up to his interpretation. "But before I forget to say this, thank you. It was an absolutely wonderful weekend."

"I'm glad you enjoyed it."

"You never talk about your family. I guess I just assumed you were fostered or something like that."

"I lived on my own for long time. I don't really remember a lot about growing up. I guess a shrink would say I blocked it out to protect myself. But I think it's more like childhood just wasn't that pleasant."

"I'm sorry."

"That was a long time ago."

"But Clair and Elwood seem like such wonderful people."

"Yes, they are. But they're not my real parents."

"They're not?"

"No."

He called them Mom and Dad, but apparently she'd assumed wrong. She waited for him to say more about his real parents, but he didn't. "It's obvious they had a major impact on your life. They're really warm and generous people. I liked them."

"They liked you, too."

She turned and looked out to sea and mused. "Every child should have wonderful memories of growing up."

"Do you remember when we talked about having a child together?" he asked.

She smiled and looked back at him. It was a memory she seldom thought about anymore. "Yes. It was the first night we met. We didn't use protection that night. I didn't expect to…"

"Neither did I, but we did."

"And I didn't get pregnant."

"But had you, she or he would be about four years old now. I often wonder what they would be like, what we would be like as parents together." Their conversation lapsed as each began to wonder, what if?

"Okay, about the interview…" she began a few minutes later.

"I hope you're going to say you'll do it."

"Actually I have a few more questions first."

"Okay," he said with ease.

"Why did you ask me? Any reporter would give a month's pay for this opportunity. You have friends throughout the media world. Why would you ask me to do this?"

"Because there's something else I'd like to ask of you."

She took a deep breath preparing for what was

coming next. It was the other shoe she'd been expecting since he came to her that first time. "What is it?"

"There's a lot of misinformation out there about me. I've been thinking about setting the record straight, about having my biography written."

"And of course you thought of me," she said dryly.

"Yes, as a matter of fact, I did."

"After everything between us and after what happened with Mason you want me to write a book about your life."

"Yes."

"I'd say it was sun stroke, but we haven't been out that long. So, I'm going to go with temporary insanity because I can't think of a single reason you'd want me, of all people, to write it or why I would even consider doing it."

"Can't you? It makes perfect sense to me. Yes, given our history, who else could be so brutally honest about everything?"

"Admittedly it would be an interesting challenge. I seldom pass up an interesting challenge."

"See, this is sounding better all the time."

"Okay, I'll do the article, but that's it."

"Excellent. Thank you. When do we get started?"

"How about right now," she said, but what she didn't say was she had started when he first mentioned it days ago. "Do you have any particular direction you'd like to focus on, the music, the businesses or perhaps your personal life?"

"You choose."

"Exactly how long is the article supposed to be?"

"That's up to you."

She nodded. "I'm going down below to get my notebook to make some notes."

"Okay, we'll be docking soon."

She looked around. "Are we near Martha's Vineyard already?"

"No, not yet, I'm going to dock off at Tucketnut Island for lunch. There's a nice little cove I'd like to show you."

"Okay." Tia went down below and began writing notes from her weekend trip with Spencer. Since he didn't have a particular direction, she wanted to focus on his personal life. She sat and started jotting down ideas and notes from the weekend centering on his love of sailing and how it derived from his early days in Central Park. It wasn't until he called down did she realize the boat was on calm water.

"Hey, how about taking a break?" he said.

She looked at her cell phone. She'd been in the cabin writing for almost an hour. "Sounds good," she called up and then stopped, hearing someone walk across the deck. "Hey, who's steering the boat?" she asked, hurrying to the steps. The cabin hatch faced the two steering wheels. Spencer wasn't at either one. She turned around seeing him walking down the side of the boat to the front. "Wait, where are you going?"

"Swimming," he said removing his shirt as he walked.

She looked up and around. There was a coastline not too far away. The boat was still, the sails were wrapped tight and everything looked secure. "Swimming, where?" she said, looking around seeing him at the bow of the boat. He took off his boat shoes and shorts. He stood naked at the bow. "Wait, you're going swimming here?" She quickly followed, but by the time she got to the bow he was standing beyond the rail. "Spencer." He dived into the water. She ran to him. The splash was clean and neat. Her jaw dropped. She looked into the blue water. She didn't see him. She panicked instantly. "Spencer! Spencer!" she called out. Then she saw bubbles and an instant later he popped up, breathing hard and smiling as he swam to the rope in the water. "What is wrong with you?"

"Come on in. It feels fantastic," he said.

"Are you insane? You can't just dive off the side of a boat like that. What if you got hurt or something?"

"I'm not hurt." He turned and swam farther out, then stopped. She saw his perfectly shaped rear near the water's surface. "Come on in," he called out again.

She stood with her hands folded over her chest defiantly. The man had a way of enticing her to do just about anything. She kicked off her shoes, removed her shirt and slipped out of her shorts. Lastly, she pulled her hair back then removed her bra and panties. She turned, seeing him watching her and smiling. "Is it cold?" she asked.

"Come on, dive in and see for yourself."

She took a deep breath, nodded and dived in. As soon as she came back up to the surface she squealed. It was chilly. She looked around for Spencer and saw him swimming toward her. As soon as he got there, she splashed him. "You are in so much trouble," she said. Spencer chuckled. "This water's freezing."

"It's not freezing. It's not the Caribbean or the Gulf, but it's definitely not the Antarctic."

She looked back at the boat. She didn't see a ladder or steps. "How do I get back on?" she asked, pushing off to swim back to the side.

"The stern, the boarding ladder's down."

She swam around to the back and saw the ladder midway in the water. She grabbed the rail and stepped up on the rung, then turned. All of the sudden the water didn't seem as cold as it did before. She dipped back down and swan back to him.

"Change your mind?" he asked.

"Actually I had a better idea." She kissed him, and they slowly sank below the surface.

Chapter 13

Foreplay while swimming naked in the Atlantic Ocean was a notch above exciting. It was sensuous, arousing and erotic. They swam, they touched, they caressed, they kissed and they played. When they finally climbed back on deck they made love right there. He tossed the cushions and pillows on the floor and entered her almost immediately. It was fast and intense and they barely got a condom on. He pounded down, she pushed up, he surged in, and she thrust forward. Together they were ravenous. They abandoned all gentile formality and instead sought the heat of pure unrestrained, uninhibited passion. In doing so, their release was nothing short of mind-blowing ecstasy. She screamed. He shouted. Their bodies shivered and twitched and then stilled in rigid elation. He rolled over, pulling her to his side. She closed her eyes and dozed off. The warmth of the sun dried them as they lay naked and in love.

She awoke lazily, feeling him carrying her to bed. Then moments later she opened her eyes, hearing the shower begin. She got up and joined him. They made love again, this time it was slow and arousing. The warmth of the water poured over their bodies as he held her up and she straddled him, wrapping her legs around his hips. He pressed her back against the wall, letting their passion take them again.

Hours later, they dressed and ate the lunch Claire packed for them. Afterward, Tia went back out on deck while Spencer stayed and cleaned the galley. He came up a few minutes later carrying dessert. "For you," he said handing her a chocolate cupcake as he sat up on the rail behind her.

"What, no French vanilla ice cream to go with it?" she joked, leaning back between his legs comfortably.

"Nah, I'll make sure to get you some when I get back," he said. She sighed. He stroked her hair, then kissed her temple. Something changed in her. "What's wrong?" he whispered.

"Going back," she said. "I don't want to go."

"Me, either," he leaned down and kissed her temple. "Unfortunately we don't have much choice. When do you have to go back to London?"

"I'm leaving for London at the end of the month.

But I'm going to Key West a few days before that. My cousin's pregnant."

"That gives us just next week."

"No, the end of this week *and* next week," she corrected.

"No, I have to go to L.A. when we get back to Martha's Vineyard."

She turned around and looked up at him. "For how long?"

"Hopefully just until the end of the week." She nodded. He leaned down again and nuzzled her neck. "Come with me. It'll be great. When's the last time you were in L.A.?"

"It's been a while."

"Then come, join me."

"No, you have business to take care of and so do I."

"I won't be working twenty-four hours a day. You can stay at the house—shop, swim, write and lounge around all day, then we can make love all night."

"That sounds tempting, but, no, my sister's coming to the island in a few days and I want to spend some time with her."

"Of course, but if you change your mind, call me. I still have the same cell phone number."

She nodded. They sat in silence for a while. He massaged her neck and shoulders and gently raked his fingers through her hair. She closed her eyes and nearly melted with contentment. "There are a lot of boats here. Where did they all come from?"

"Mostly from Nantucket," he said. "A lot of them came for the regattas then stay around the rest of the week. This area sometimes turns into a lover's lane at night."

She smiled. "Is this how you seduce all your *friends,* Mr. Cage?"

"Only the ones I'm in love with, Ms. Coles." She went still. "Yes, I said it. I love you. I never stopped."

She stood up and walked away. "Spencer, we can't do this."

He followed and stood behind her, his arms around her waist. "Tia, I don't have a choice. You are forever my one and only love. There's no denying it. From the moment we touched, there was no turning back for me. I love you."

"Spencer…"

"No, don't say anything now. I just wanted you to know how I feel. I don't want this to ever be over."

The words, *we may not have a choice,* burned in her thoughts, but she didn't say them. She didn't say anything. Not because she didn't want to or didn't love him—she did, more than he'd ever know. But because she knew what yielding to the truth of her feelings would do to her heart if this was over. She couldn't take another heartbreak like before. So the beauty of the moment had to pass her by. She looked out, seeing a heavy mist roll in. "It looks like it's about to get foggy," she said. "Maybe we're better get out of here."

"No, we can't now. There are too many boats around

us. It would be like sailing blind in bumper cars. We'll have to stay here until it clears."

Tia wrapped her arms around her body and continued looking out into the approaching night. She watched the silent fog ease in and thicken as it closed in around them. After a while it was impossible to see anything, even the boats closest to them were shrouded in mist. Tia looked around nervously. There was a hushed silence in the air. "It feels so eerie," she whispered.

He looked around. "It's just low-hanging clouds."

"I know, but it feels strange, like we're the only people on the planet. It's so quiet and still." Just then they heard the sound of a woman shriek repeatedly in pleasure. Her moans got louder and louder then she screamed a man's name at the top of her lungs. Tia turned to Spencer. "Was that what I think it was?" she asked.

He nodded. "If you think it was a woman being made love to in the fog, then, yes, you'll hear a lot of that pretty soon. There's something extremely sexual and seductive about making love in public while covered by a thick fog."

"Really?" she said. He nodded. "Have you ever…"

"No."

"Ever been tempted?"

He smiled. "Like right now?"

"Yes, like right now."

That's all it took for the moment to take hold and their passions to erupt. He kissed her and she opened her heart to him, holding nothing back. They made love on the boat, on the deck, surrounded by dense, blanketed fog for none to see. Everything they were feeling intensified with every intimate movement. Then, with eyes open, they watched as the slow and seductive rapturous release came and seemed to shake the planet. In ecstasy, they soared above the waves. Afterward, breathless in surrender, they held each other, molding their bodies as one. "Spencer Cage, you're a remarkable man," she said softly.

"No, I'm not," he said quickly, feeling the pain of his past actions ripping at his heart. He'd long since given up his plan to seduce the stock shares from her. All he wanted now was her by his side forever. Everything in the world he ever wanted, he'd found in her arms. He loved her fiercely with passion and unconditional surrender. "I'm a man who wants something."

"Tell me what you want?" she asked.

"I want you."

She smiled happily. "Good answer, and right now you have me."

"No, that's not good enough. I want all of you."

"Spencer…"

"Love me. Marry me, Tatiana. I want to fall asleep with you every night and wake up with you in my arms every morning. I want to make love to you six times a day until I'm ninety-nine years old and even then I want more."

"Spencer…" she began.

"Yes, I'm proposing to you. I'm not going to let you walk out of my life again."

"Spencer, I…"

"Shhh, it's okay. Don't answer me now. We'll talk when I get back. Just think about it, and then…"

"I know the rest," she said softly.

"…say yes," he finished his sentence anyway.

She closed her eyes. Her carefree vacation romance had turned into something unexpectedly real.

Chapter 14

Martha's Vineyard seemed like foreign soil by the time they arrived back. It had only been five days, but it might as well have been five decades. Everything seemed so different. She was so different. She was in love. She had slept better than she had in months. The gentle sway of the boat and Spencer's warm, naked body pressed to hers kept her in perfect peace all night. After making love on deck they had gone down below and slept together. The fears were gone and so were the nightmares. All she felt was love. Even now, days later, she smiled, contented.

Their last night together on the boat was incredible. It was like the universe aligned to give her one perfect gift. She closed her eyes and took a deep breath, then slowly exhaled. The impulse to smile swept over her again as it had for the last few days. And why not? She was deliriously happy. Everything was right with the world. Spencer had told her he loved her and had asked her to marry him. Just thinking about his words made her heart beat faster and her stomach flutter.

He had opened his heart to her and now she chided herself for not telling him the truth of how she felt, too. She should have told him she loved him, but she couldn't. She was afraid. Saying it out loud to him meant she'd be giving him a part of her she long held in protective care. But in her heart she knew it was already too late for that. She had fallen in love with Spencer Cage a long, long time ago. And now she was ready to give everything to him.

After they arrived at the harbor he dropped her off at the house. They said their goodbyes and then he was gone. Now, four days later, she was still thinking about that night. The short trip he initially planned to L.A. had turned into a few extra days in Atlanta, as well. She kept busy by writing the article on him. They talked throughout the day. She asked questions and he answered. Then at night they had long, seductive conversations about their hopes and dreams. At one point they attempted to have phone sex, but both of them opted instead to wait until they were together again.

Maybe she should have taken him up on his offer and traveled to L.A. with him. But she knew she'd get nothing done and neither would he. Also, she expected her sister, Niki, to arrive soon, but she didn't. She ran into some unexpected problems with her café expansion. She promised to be there in another few days. It didn't matter now. Spencer was coming back and she was going to say yes.

After a quick swim Tia dried herself off, wrapped her waist with her sarong and relaxed back down on the towel-covered chair she arranged on the terrace earlier. She didn't particularly like swimming in the ocean, and she knew the Sullivans wouldn't mind her using their pool. Her dip was just quick enough to cool herself off. Although the sun was shining brightly and the temperature had to be well over eighty degrees, it wasn't the weather that was making her so hot. It was thoughts of Spencer's return tomorrow.

"Okay, enough of this. It's time to focus, girl," she said out loud. She opened her laptop and began editing her first draft. She'd just reworked the first few paragraphs when her email message beeped. She expected it to be Spencer. It wasn't. It was Greer emailing her about the outline she sent him two days ago. He loved the direction she'd chosen. He forwarded his notes and a request for any photos she might have taken to go with the article.

She went back in the house and grabbed her camera's memory card and inserted it into the computer slot. She pressed a few keys and numerous photos came up, including those she'd recently taken while in Nantucket. She chose a few of her favorites and uploaded them to

Greer with her response. Then instead of going back to work she continued flipping through the photos. Her email beeped. It was Greer again. He was in an editorial meeting and showed her photos. By unanimous decision, they wanted to offer her the feature article and front page photo in the next issue.

"Oh, my God! I got the cover, I got the cover," she exclaimed excitedly. She quickly began typing an email to tell Spencer the good news. Then she deleted it and decided to tell him when he arrived the following day. They could celebrate that along with her accepting his marriage proposal. She forwarded a copy of Greer's email to Pam, her agent. This news motivated her to refocus and get back to work. Front cover meant the article had to be absolutely perfect. As soon as she started typing a shadow crossed the computer's screen. Startled, she looked up and turned around.

"So, this is where you've been hiding out."

She removed her sunglasses to see Donavan standing above her. Even though he had on dark shades she could feel his eyes all over her body. "Damn, girl, you look too sexy lying there like that. Shame, we could have been so good together."

"Hello, Donavan," she said, still too happy about her news to be annoyed with him showing up at the cottage unannounced. "I thought you were in L.A."

"I was. But I decided to come back early. I missed you. So, is that all I get? Just a 'hello, Donavan'?"

"What do you want?" she asked.

"How about a kiss?" he said, smiling seductively.

"What do you want?" she repeated.

"A'ight, a'ight, you want to get to the business thing, that's fine. Let's get straight to it." He sat down in the chair beside her, uninvited. "I come bearing gifts." She saved her file and closed her laptop. "All right, here it is. Portman told me you're not interested in selling the shares Mason left you."

"That's right, I'm not."

"I think you need to change your mind."

"Why would I want to do that?"

"I told you before I have deep pockets. I can make it worth your while."

"I have enough money."

"Oh, so you think you're gonna wait for Spencer to offer you more? I don't think so. He doesn't have it."

"Spencer hasn't offered me anything. And besides, he owns the company. He doesn't need my shares."

Donavan laughed out loud. "Girl, you have no idea what you have, do you? Mason gave you one third of SCE stock. Spencer has one third. The rest of us share the rest. When you sell me your shares, I control the company."

"What?"

"What do you think he's been doing all this time? He's using you to get the shares. Hell, at least I was up-front about it. I wasn't trying to screw you out of them, literally."

"You're lying," she said, not believing him.

"Am I?" he said sarcastically. "You got an offer to buy your shares from Frank McDermott, right?" he said. She didn't respond either way. "Frank is Spencer's personal attorney. He's been playing you all this time. Let me guess, he told you he loved you. He wants to marry you. Don't you know he'd say anything to keep his company, and since Mason left you those shares it ain't gonna happen. If you asked me, I'd say it's his way of getting revenge for what he thinks you did to Mason, but I could be wrong."

She was fuming but kept her temper and rage under control. There was no way she wanted Donavan to know she was getting played. "Is that all?" she said, putting her sunglasses back on and opening her laptop again.

"So, are we doing business or what? I've got a record label behind me. My dad's a VP. I'm holding all the cards. When I take over, I'll take care of you."

"You're taking over Spencer's company?"

"That's right."

"I thought he was supposed to be your friend."

"Yo, like they say, it's not personal. This is business."

"And this is personal—goodbye, Donavan. I have work to do."

"A'ight, think about what I said and call Portman back." He got up and paused a moment before walking away. "Damn, you do look good lying there."

She ignored him just long enough for him to walk away. But as much as she wanted to, she couldn't ignore what he said. She didn't respond. She didn't have to. She knew he was lying. Still her heart struggled with her doubts. She knew without a doubt she was in love with Spencer. She never stopped loving him. But a nudge of concern needled her. Frank McDermott had definitely called her. He told her he represented an investor interesting in buying her shares. If that was the truth, why would Donavan lie about everything else?

She pressed a key and the screen on her laptop came to life. The photos of Spencer came up again. She looked at them feeling her heart begin to sink. What if Donavon was telling the truth? What if Spencer had just been using her to get what he really wanted? Could he really be that cruel? She typed in Frank's name. His company website came up. She read through his site not seeing anything particularly telling. He was just a high-powered attorney. She went to his internet images page.

She often checked out a person's images page to see who their friends might be. There were numerous photos of Frank, of course, she expected that. There were a few with some of his clients and close friends. She continued searched, then found what made her heart stop for an instant. "Oh, my God."

She read the caption, then closed the laptop. She got up and walked back into the house. She showered and changed her clothes then went down to the beach and started walking. It was the night of the Grand Illumination. Houses all along the beach and through the streets of Oak Bluffs were aglow with paper and plastic lanterns. She barely noticed. Her mind swirled in a million different directions. He had used her. She looked around. The sun was gone and rain clouds threatened to cover the sky. It wasn't far enough. She kept walking. It wasn't until she got to the lighthouse did she realize how far she'd gone. She sat down on the side and watched the waves crest against the rocks. How could she be so wrong, again?

Spencer was physically and mentally exhausted. He had just spent four days in L.A. and two days in Atlanta. Still, all he could think about was getting back to Martha's Vineyard and seeing Tia. His private plane had just landed. He got in his car and headed to the small cottage. Six days was far more time than he wanted to spend away from her, but he needed to attend to business. He was hands-on when it came to every facet of his company. Yet Tia stayed in his thoughts the whole time. She was his addiction and being away from her for too long was making him crazy.

While he drove he listened as his attorney, Frank McDermott, explain his legal options. Unfortunately, the meeting they had in L.A. didn't go as well as he expected. There were investors lining up, but he didn't want their money. The more people he had on board, the more problems he knew he'd have later on. Cage Enterprises was making money and everybody wanted some. A large major label, International Media Group, was his main concern right now. They wanted to buy him out, but keep him as CEO. There was no way he was doing that. He saw what they did to BoomBox when Mason had to sell to them. They cut it up and went public. The company folded a year later. Now they were after him and SCE.

"Any headway on buying the shares?" Spencer asked.

"She hasn't returned my requests for a meeting. I don't know where she stands. It looks like she could go either way, keep them or sell them. The problem is to whom. Drill mentioned you were trying another angle."

"No, not anymore," he said.

"Okay, if the record label does succeed, you're looking at a very nice payout and a lot less work on your part. You'll be president without the full management responsibilities. The major label takes the hit, pros and cons. They've officially put an offer on the table. They're naming Donavon Reynolds as CEO. The company name will change, but they assure us nothing else will at this point. It's not bad at all. All of you can walk away very wealthy. Flip side, you pass on the president's position and after a few years start again."

"No. I'm not starting over again."

"Okay, then you need to make sure Ms. Coles doesn't sell her shares and everything will stay exactly the same," Frank said. "Drill told me you had a relationship with Ms. Coles. Perhaps you could tell her the precarious position you're in. After all, she is part of the company, too."

"No."

"Okay, your call. Do you want me to continue pressing her?"

"No, let it go. Thanks, Frank, I'll talk to you later."

He disconnected the speakerphone call as he pulled into his driveway. After the three-and-a-half-hour flight from Atlanta he intended to freshen up before going to see Tia. She actually expected him back tomorrow, but he couldn't wait another day. He saw Drill's car parked out front.

"Yo," he called out as soon as he entered the house. There was no answer. That meant Drill was probably in the soundproof studio downstairs. He went upstairs, showered and changed then headed to the studio. He opened the door, walked in but stayed in the back. As expected, Drill was sitting at the board with his headphones on. Spencer picked up his headphones to listen. Drill had edited and remixed his two tracks. They were perfect.

When the last song went off they greeted each other. "Man, that was excellent. I talked to production and marketing while I was in L.A. We need to get them a master copy. They want to do a limited online release to coincide with Tia's interview."

"I bet they're thrilled she showed up. You see Donavan?" Drill asked.

"No. Why, is he here?"

"Yeah, he just left. He said he saw Tia. They talked. If she finds out what you've been doing from Donavan, she's going to be furious."

"I gotta talk to her now. The label made the offer."

"Damn. What you gonna do, man?"

"I can't just roll over and I can't lose Tia."

"A'ight, then go do what you gotta do."

"Drill, do you have any idea why Mason would leave her the shares and not me?"

"He owed you, man. It was his way of paying you back."

"I don't understand."

Drill shook his head. "You saw Mason as some great guy. Yeah, he was cool and all but had his drama, too. As soon as he saw you and Tia together he knew you wouldn't be around long. He needed you. You were the future of BoomBox and he knew it. He used to say Tia bewitched you. Man, he hated her guts about that."

"What?" Spencer said, shocked to hear this.

"Oh, yeah, he did everything he could to break you two up. Nothing worked. Ya'll just got closer. Then when you were talking marriage he knew he had to do something major. Who do you think was her source for the book?"

"Donavon," he said.

"Nah, man, Mason was his own source. Why do you think he never tried to sue her over it? She had all kinds of shit on him. He gave her everything. The thing is, I was always surprised she held back. She could have had him in jail for the rest of his life, but she didn't because of you. Then when the book came out you broke up. That's all Mason wanted."

"Why didn't you tell me this before?"

"I'm telling you now," Drill said. Spencer glared at him hard. He nodded. "A'ight. I promised him I'd take it to my grave. But the reason he gave her the shares was to even the score. He was trying to make it right. He called her and they talked. He even called that night when she was in Istanbul. A few days later he was dead."

"I gotta go."

Spencer ran down the beach to the cottage. Tia wasn't there. He stood on the terrace looking up and down the beach for her. Then he saw her in the far off distance walking toward the lighthouse. He followed, hoping to catch up with her. When he got to the lighthouse he found her sitting and staring out at the ocean. "Tia." She turned around and looked at him. "Your shares, the ones Mason gave you. Are you going to sell them to Donavon?"

"I don't know. I haven't thought about it. Why?" She looked into his eyes. They said it all. Right then she knew what Donavan told her was true. Her heart was crushed. "Everything was a lie, wasn't it?" she said.

He walked over to her. "No, not everything. My love for you wasn't."

"Love? You don't know what love is."

"I know I love you and can't live without you in my life."

She laughed. "Oh, please, you can stop pretending

now. I know all you want from me is my signature to save your company."

"No, if it means losing you, I don't want it. Sell them, keep them, I don't care. I just want you. I love you, Tia. That's all I care about."

"So what exactly was the plan? Convince me you wanted me and even marry me to get them?"

He looked away ashamed of his actions. But he wasn't going to lie to her. "That's how it started, yes. But at the party when we danced, that first night I knew I still loved you. It's not about the company now. It's about me and you together."

"I opened my heart to you and you did this to me. Why? Donavon said it was revenge because of the book."

"No, never."

"You asked me to trust you. I did. You asked me to love you, I did. How could you do this to me?" Her eyes burned with tears of pain as they blazed. "You almost cost me everything." He looked at her confused. "Oh, please. Don't tell me you didn't know your attorney and his corporate executive client are suing me and the company I work for. What does he get out of it?"

"Tia, Frank is my attorney, yes. I had him call you about selling your shares but that's it. I'm not privy to his cases with other clients. I had no idea they even knew each other."

"I saw a photo of them hanging out together."

"I didn't know. All I know is that I love you. I always did and I always will."

"You don't know what love is. Love is telling me the truth about your life, all of it."

"You want to know my life, the real me. Okay, here's the real me, my dad's in jail. He's been there all my life. He'll be there until the day he dies. And my mom, well, she's on drugs. In my whole life I've never seen her clean. I was born on drugs. They had to detox me just so I could live. That's my real life. My mom and dad, neither situation is going to change anytime soon. My grandmother raised me. When she died, I raised me. I was living on the streets when I met Mason. He got me to contact my aunt Claire and uncle Elwood. Mason didn't just help me, he saved my life. He took a bullet for me. I owed him."

"Do you think I ever cared about your past or who you parents were? All I wanted was for you to love me and trust me."

"Tatiana…"

"And as for the shares Mason willed to me, I don't care about them, either. I never did. They just sat there. But, yeah, I know exactly why he gave them to me. They were his conscience. But you take them, they're yours. Free of charge. Maybe now you'll trust our love."

"Tatiana, I sacrificed our love for nothing. I risked it all and threw us away. I turned my back on the one thing I needed, you. I can't do it again. Don't go."

"I love you, too, but just like before, I'm walking

away." She backed up, turned around and started back to the cottage. It seemed to take forever to get there. When she finally climbed the stairs to the terrace, she turned. Spencer was nowhere in sight. She walked into the cottage and stopped cold.

"Surprise!" Natalia, Nikita and Mia were in the kitchen holding up glasses of champagne. Their smiles filled her with love. She burst into tears of sorrow and joy. They surrounded her instantly. She told them what had been happening. They hugged and held her close. "I'm so happy to see all of you," Tia said tearfully, "but right now I just want to leave this island."

"Nat," Nikita said to her sister.

Natalia nodded and grabbed her phone from her purse. She called someone and arrangements were made instantly. Two hours later, the same private plane that had brought them was headed back to Key West.

Chapter 15

Tia spent all morning hanging out at her sister's Teen Center. She met with a roomful of students from local high schools interested in writing and communications as college majors. She talked to them about the business, gave tips and suggestions and finally answered questions about her life and her career. Most were centered on who she knew and where she'd been. They were very impressed that she had traveled so extensively, but not so much by the men and women she interviewed.

"So when you travel all around the world, how do you get to have a boyfriend and what about having kids?"

She smiled tightly. "Truthfully, it's difficult. Being a journalist isn't easy and sometimes you have to make sacrifices for what you really want. When you choose a career path like mine, you don't always get to have lasting relationships." There were discouraged murmurs around the room. "But," she began again, hoping she hadn't completely disheartened them, "that doesn't mean you can't have a family and children. A lot of my friends and coworkers in the business are very successful with both a career and family."

"Are you married?" a teenager asked.

"No."

"Are you in a relationship?" another teen asked.

"No, not at the moment," she said slowly.

"What about writing books? Mrs. Morales and Mrs. Montgomery said you wrote a book before about Mason Brooks the rapper."

She nodded. "Yes, I did. That was a few years ago."

"What was it like meeting him?"

"Mason was an interesting character." She said the words and realized it was the same response she gave Spencer weeks ago. "I enjoyed my time with him and his friends."

"You mean his friends like Spencer Cage?" someone asked. Tia's heart jumped.

"Ohh, I love me some Cage," a young girl quickly responded. "The man is gorgeous and so sexy."

"Yeah, and he can sing, too. I heard he's going back in the studio to record a new CD."

"Yeah, yeah, I heard that, too."

"Nah, I like Donavan better. He's bad-boy hot."

Tia let them talk freely about the men she knew too

well, especially Spencer. She smiled and nodded as they made all kinds of wild assumptions, some fact, others nowhere near the truth. With all the talk around her she never said a word either way. After a while they began asking questions about other entertainers she'd met and then about world leaders. The conversation went on for another five minutes. Then she finally got them back to talking about journalism. When the program was over she took a few more questions before leaving. She was supposed to stay longer, but she really needed to get out of there.

"You were incredible. They loved you," Mia gushed.

"I think they were more impressed with who I knew and where I've been."

"Doesn't matter, they loved it all. Are you staying?"

"No, I'm going over to Niki's place to get something to eat. Do you want anything?"

"No, thanks. I'm still queasy in the mornings. I have a box of crackers and tea. That'll hold me until later."

"You mean later as in at my going away party?" Tia asked.

Mia's jaw dropped. "How did you know? Who told you?"

Tia smiled, waved and walked out hearing her cousin calling her name for answers. The truth was she didn't know for sure until Mia just confirmed it. But she'd never tell her that.

She got into her sister's car and drove into town to the café. She parked across the street and walked over, speaking to a few people she knew on the way. As soon as she walked into the storefront she felt so much better. The afternoon rush was over and only a few local patrons remained. She placed an order for a cup of tea and some freshly baked sugar cookies. Afterward she went into the kitchen. Niki was standing at the stove with her hand on her hip while stirring something in a large pot. Her assistant was there with her schedule book open. "Hey, what's going on?" Tia asked.

"Tell him no, absolutely not. I don't care how much he's paying us, tell him I'm not doing it," Niki said, then turned around to see her sister standing there. "Can you believe this? Now he wants to change the menu a week and a half before the event? The man is crazy and he's driving me crazy, too."

Tia shook her head. This was her sister's world. She knew Niki loved what she did, drama and all. She also knew no matter how much she complained, she'd have whatever it was perfect and delicious and right on time. "You okay?"

"Yes, I'm fine, my client is just nerve-racking."

"You look busy. I just stopped by to grab some cookies for the boys. I'll see you later." She shook her head, grabbed her tea and cookies, then left.

An hour later she watched her nephews play in the backyard while her sister ran some errands. The simple joy of seeing their happy faces seemed to make her feel so much better.

The truth was she intended to make herself as content

as possible with her new life. She sent in the interview with Spencer and was extremely proud of what she did. Greer was thrilled. He wanted to lead with Spencer at the helm of his boat on the cover with the copy, *The New Spencer Cage* as the heading.

"Hey, girl," Nat said, coming outside with Mia behind her.

"Hey, so where's the party going to be? Here or at Niki's place in town."

"See, told you she knew," Mia said.

"It's the reporter in her. It's here and it's not anything big, just a small going away party."

"Actually, I've been thinking about that. I once told Pam I wanted to start my own website. So, I've been researching it. I think that's what I'm going to do. I'm staying. I'm coming back home." Nat and Mia delighted in her news. Brice and Jayden soon joined in. "Wait, wait, I'm not staying right now. I still have to go back to London and sell my apartment and quit my job and do a million other things."

"But you're coming home, that's all that matters," Nat said happily as she and Mia sat down with her. "How are you feeling?" Mia asked.

Tia nodded and half smiled. "Better. I'll be fine."

"Tia, you have to resolve this. You love that man. It's all over your face and I have a feeling he loves you just as much. Yes, he made mistakes. Yes, screwed up and yes, he was wrong. He was trying to save his company and he was trying to love you," Nat said.

"She's right," Mia added. "Love makes us do crazy, mindless things. But love also helps us to open our heart and forgive. You knew what Stephen and I went through before we said I do."

"Yeah, and what about me and David? We wouldn't have had a chance at this wonderful life we have now. You love him, he loves you. There's nothing more amazing than that."

Tia nodded. They were right. She did love Spencer with all her heart. "I'll think about it."

"Good, now come on. Let's get ready for this, *not* going away party we're throwing you. Niki's sending the food, but she's going to be a little late." They got up and headed back to the house.

Spencer got off the private plane in Key West. David Montgomery, his good friend, met him at the hangar. The two men shook hands and greeted each other. "Thanks, man. I appreciate this. Are you sure this isn't going to get you in trouble with your wife when she finds out?"

"She already knows. There's no way I'd do this without her knowing. But don't worry, Nat's wonderful. Once you fix this, everything will be fine. You had just better fix this," he emphasized strongly as they climbed into his jeep.

Spencer sat down and nodded in all seriousness. He had every intention of not only fixing this, but leaving Key West with Tia at his side. "I definitely will."

"Did I mention my grandfather-in-law is a sheriff,

my cousin is a deputy and my wife has her badge, as well? She's an excellent markswoman. Never misses what she aims for."

"I guess I'd better be careful around her."

"Actually, she's not the sister you need to watch out for. Niki's a master chef. She has sharp knives and she knows how to use them. She makes things disappear. You seriously don't want to get on her bad side," David added. Spencer looked at him anxiously, then, seeing the levity in his eyes, relaxed. David chuckled. "Come on, man, relax. You'll be fine. I know you love her and she loves you."

Spencer shook his head smiling. "I know. It's just that I've waited so long to be right here, right now. It seems like everything in my life so far has been leading up to this one point. We've missed out on our lives together for so long and I love her so much."

David smiled knowing how much he loved his wife. "You're here to be with the woman you love, how great is that?"

They drove through town and to the outskirts of Key West talking about marriage and how David's life had changed after becoming a husband and father. They pulled up in front of his new home. There were numerous cars already parked in the large driveway. "There's a gazebo along this path. Wait there, I'll have Nat ask her to go to the gazebo."

Spencer nodded. He got out and started walking down the lit path to wait as David instructed. A few minutes later he heard the back door open. He turned and saw Tia. She looked beautiful. "Okay, I'll get it, but why on earth did you leave it in the gazebo?" she asked, then closed the door and started walking toward him.

"Tia," he said softly.

She stopped walking. "Spencer?"

"Yes."

"What are you doing here?"

"Trusting our love," he said.

She recognized the words. They were hers, the last ones she spoke to him before she left him at the lighthouse. "Spencer…"

"Tia, after you left three years ago I thought I could get through my life just fine without you. Then when I saw you on the beach, I realized I hadn't been living at all. I was just hanging around waiting to breathe again. As soon as I saw you I knew."

"Spencer…"

"I can't wait another three years or another three seconds. I need you in my life now, right now. I love you. Nothing and no one can change that, not even me. I love Tatiana Coles, with all my heart and with all my soul I love you."

Tia looked into his eyes and saw everything she ever needed to see. She saw her future, his past and their life together. She loved him. "Spencer…"

"I was wrong. I tried to save my company and keep the woman I love and I realized I couldn't do both. Nothing is as important to me as you being in my life.

I don't care about the company. As a matter of fact I'm selling my shares."

"Are you crazy? You can't do that. Do you really want Donavon in charge?"

"If it means losing you again, I don't care. He can have it. All I want is you, now and forever."

"Well, you can't sell."

"Actually I can, I was thinking about moving to London or maybe going to Madagascar and hanging around on the beach for a while."

"No, I need the money. I'm going to publish my own online news magazine right here in the States."

His eyes immediately lit up. "You're staying here?" She nodded. "You're staying here in the States, for real?"

She nodded and smiled. "Yes, I think it's time I came back home. Although I'm not quite sure where home is going to be right now. Where do you suggest we live?"

He smiled wide. "Wherever you are is where I am."

She couldn't help but smile. She shook her head. "I love you," she said quietly.

"I love you." He reached into his pocket and pulled out a small ring box. "I bought this the morning after we met. I knew right then, you were my heart." He opened the box and pulled a ring out to show her.

Tears of joy welled in her eyes. "It's perfect."

"Tatiana Coles, will you marry me?"

She nodded happily and wrapped her arms around his neck and held tight. "Yes, yes, yes."

There was suddenly loud, riotous cheering as everybody at the party stood at the windows and doors celebrating their love. Spencer and Tia looked back, smiled and laughed. She was deliriously happy. He kissed her and the outside garden lights turned on. It was magical. It was heavenly. It was love. Forever.

* * * * *

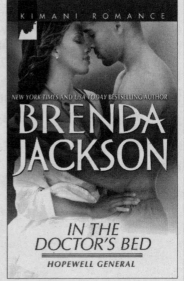

REQUEST YOUR FREE BOOKS!

2 FREE NOVELS PLUS 2 FREE GIFTS!

KIMANI™
ROMANCE

Love's ultimate destination!

KROM11B

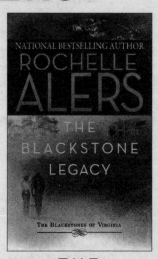